THE HOUSE OF WIDOWS

THE FAMILY OF WILLIAM NEILSON BOOK IV

THE HOUSE OF WIDOWS

James Buchan

Maps © Emily Faccini

First published in Great Britain in 2025 by
Mountain Leopard Press
An imprint of HEADLINE PUBLISHING GROUP LIMITED

I

Cataloguing in Publication Data is available from the British Library

Hardback ISBN 978 1 0354 2556 3

Typeset in Adobe Caslon Pro 11.5pt/16.4pt by Six Red Marbles UK, Thetford, Norfolk

Printed and bound in Great Britain by Clays Ltd, Elcograf S.p.A.

MIX
Paper | Supporting responsible forestry
FSC
www.fsc.org   FSC® C104740

Headline's policy is to use papers that are natural, renewable and recyclable products and made from wood grown in well-managed forests and other controlled sources. The logging and manufacturing processes are expected to conform to the environmental regulations of the country of origin.

HEADLINE PUBLISHING GROUP LIMITED
An Hachette UK Company
Carmelite House
50 Victoria Embankment
London EC4Y 0DZ

The authorised representative in the EEA is Hachette Ireland,
8 Castlecourt Centre, Dublin 15, D15 XTP3, Ireland (email: info@hbgi.ie)

www.headline.co.uk
www.hachette.co.uk

CONTENTS

Quelque rare que soit le véritable amour, il l'est encore moins rare que la véritable amitié

True love may be uncommon enough, but it is still less uncommon than true friendship

Duc de La Rochefoucauld

Author's Note: *William Neilson, who narrated the first three books of this story, is dead, fallen in the French defeat at Quebec in 1759. The tale is taken up by his grandson, also William, a cadet at the Royal Military College in Paris.*

Ninnipen's short speech on page 145 is taken, word for word, from The Jesuit Relations and Allied Documents, *Vol. 55, p. 274.*

PART I

The House of Widows

I

During the later years of the eighteenth century, a respectable address in the city of Paris was the street known as rue
Varenne or de la Varenne. Running in a westwards direction,
on the south or left bank of the River Seine beyond the
Abbey of Saint-Germain-des-Prés, it had been in old times a
lane amid wastes and hunting-ground. In the passage of
years, the lands each side had been allotted and built upon
with private houses, each with its coachmen's gate, court-
yard, *corps-de-logis* or principal range, pair side-wings, and
garden laid out in the geometrical taste.

Among those houses on the south side, and not the least
superb, was the hôtel Joyeuse-Neilson. Erected by the last duc
de Joyeuse in the reign of King Louis XIV, the house had
passed out of fashion, its golden urns and blazons as apt as an
old man's leer in a gathering of chaste young persons. A
passer-by of those days remarked less its Gothick architecture

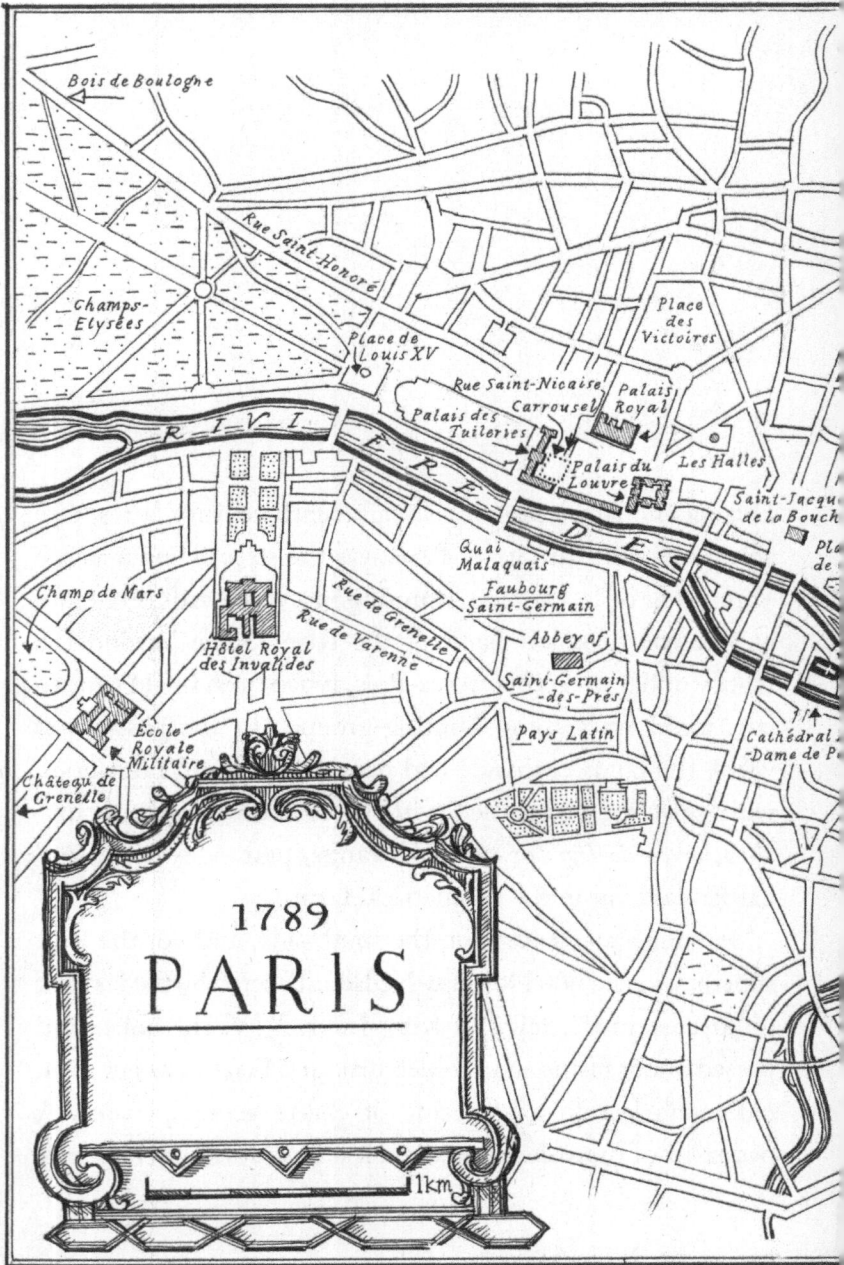

Bois de Boulogne

Rue Saint-Honoré

Champs-Elysées

Place de Louis XV

Place des Victoires

Rue Saint-Nicaise
Carrousel

Palais Royal

Palais des Tuileries

Palais du Louvre

Les Halles

RIVIERE DE

Saint-Jacques de la Bouch

Quai Malaquais

Pla de

Champ de Mars

Faubourg Saint-Germain

Rue de Grenelle

Rue de Varenne

Abbey of

Hôtel Royal des Invalides

Saint-Germain -des-Prés

École Royale Militaire

Pays Latin

Cathédral Dame de P

Château de Grenelle

1789

PARIS

1km

The environs of PARIS

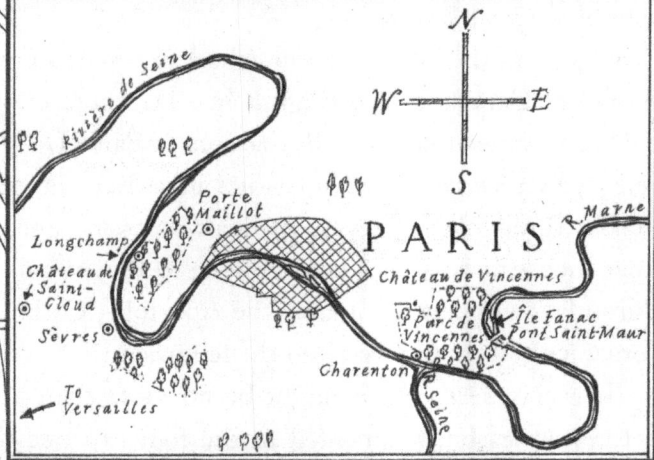

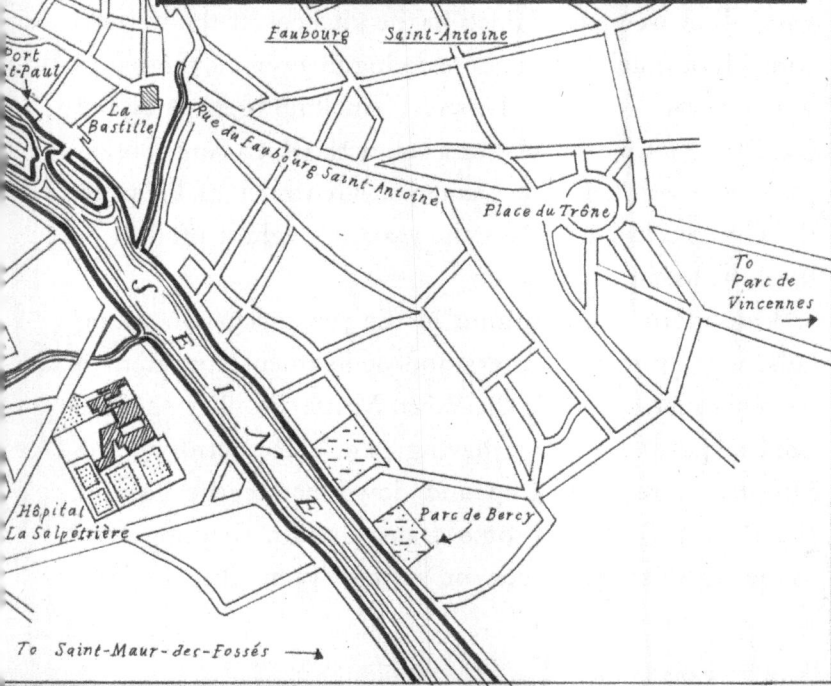

N
W E
S

PARIS

Rivière de Seine

Porte
Maillot

Longchamp

Château de
Saint-Cloud

Sèvres

R. Marne

Château de Vincennes

Parc de
Vincennes

Île Fanac
Pont Saint-Maur

Charenton

R. Seine

To
Versailles

Faubourg Saint-Antoine

Port
St-Paul

La
Bastille

Rue du Faubourg Saint-Antoine

Place du Trône

To
Parc de
Vincennes

S E I N E

Hôpital
La Salpétrière

Parc de Bercy

To Saint-Maur-des-Fossés

than the mob of Canadians and other wild folk encamped in front of the *porte-cochère*.

Subjects of the Huron nation, who had come to France at the fall of Canada to the English in 1760, those emigrants had been swelled in number by maroons of Saint-Domingue, weary galley-convicts, gallant ladies in retirement, sea-sick pirates, timid night-thieves, penitent assassins and divers other such strayed sheep, who, so long as they submitted to Huron law and custom, and to the Apostolic, Catholic and Roman cult, were received into the fellowship.

Their numbers, which might be no more than a dozen in the fair season, augmented in the foul to three or four score. They were entertained in the kitchens of the western wing of the hôtel. When not restoring themselves, those persons liked to lounge in the street, smoking their pipes and accosting foot-passengers for a sol, with which contribution they were satisfied. The Lieutenant-Generalcy of Police of the City of Paris had, over the years, thought it prudent to leave the nest untroubled.

One morning of autumn in the year 1784, two young lads, who from their dress and deportment appeared to be gentlemen-cadets of the Royal Military College a hundred steps to the west, having paid their octroi to the Hurons, were pacing up and down before the gate of the hôtel as if debating some strategic affair. They appeared to be aged some fifteen or sixteen years. Finally, the less dishevelled of the two boys, rocking on his heels, burst out:

"Did I not know it to be impossible, I'd say you was nervous, friend."

"I am not nervous, Neilson. I wished merely to gather my thoughts before broaching the threshold."

In part because they were créoles, one Scotch, one Italian, they were the best of friends. One was admired by his brother-cadets, the other shunned, and that made their friendship the more distinct.

The young men were led across the court by a North American, relayed to another, and then to a third, which last brought them into a long room overlooking a shining garden. Seated in the southern window-light, at her work, was a lady in widow's black.

"Good day, Mme Dalouhe!"

"I am not deaf, rascal. Who's blackie?"

"May I present my friend and brother cadet, M. di Buonaparte?"

William Neilson gave the family name four syllables and the Italian particle.

"Turk?"

"Corsican, my lady."

"As I said. And I am not your lady."

The conversation seemed to have reached its term, when a door opened at the end of the saloon. A lady, not young but not far gone in years, dressed alike in mourning black, entered. As she stepped into the room, the lady gave the impression of having woken from a dream of open air. The boys stood at attention. The lady smiled.

"William, you have made my day." She turned to M. Buonaparte. "Will you not present your fellow-scholar?"

"Corsican cut-throat."

"Cut-throat or not, Mme Dalouhe, any friend of my nephew is welcome here."

"Napoleone di Buonaparte, my lady. It is an honour to be presented to so famous a warrior."

"If you please, M. di Buonaparte. My fighting career was short and disgraceful."

"Pardon me, Mme Duclos, but I have heard otherwise."

"Arse-kisser!"

"Please sit, gentlemen."

M. Buonaparte obeyed, but an eye-brow from his friend set him upright. The adjustment of manoeuvre from one of sitting down to one of remaining standing was not well executed.

"But you are suffering, M. Buonaparte."

Mme Dalouhe cackled.

"It is nothing. I slipped in the fencing-school while being soundly beaten by M. Neilson."

"My tits!"

"Mme Dalouhe, would you kindly order breakfast for M. Neilson and M. di Buonaparte?"

With that request, Mme Duclos appeared to intend a double result, both supplying her beloved nephew and his friend with refreshment, and ushering Mme Dalouhe off the stage. It should be said that the speech of Mme Dalouhe had not always been so coarse. Years, widowhood and, perhaps, her companion's reticence had taken their toll. (Mme Dalouhe had quarrelled with her children, first singly, and then in troops.) The lady set off, cursing, to fulfil her charge.

"Do you drink Champagne, M. Buonaparte? My godfather, General Neilson, was devoted to Champagne."

"I have never tasted Champagne, madame."

"Then the pleasure and honour are ours."

The lady's manner was so plain, it appeared to M. di Buonaparte an affectation. Had M. di Buonaparte, of a precarious family of the city of Ajaccio, known that his hostess had been beforetimes a barefoot servant, as had Mme Dalouhe, he would not have been surprised.

"What branch of the military profession have you chosen, M. Buonaparte?"

"The artillery, madame."

"That is my brother's specialism. He has been an artillerist since the cradle. My god-father, the late General Neilson, had no particular genius: sometimes artillery, sometimes engineering, sometimes the marine. In Persia once, he captured a Russian fort before waking the defenders. He turned the tide at Carillon in Canada without firing a shot. He had, M. di Buonaparte, a touch of Scotch wizardry."

"Alas, my lady, those not so gifted must fall back on ballistics and equations."

In this house of soldiers' widows, M. Buonaparte told his friend as they sauntered back to the Champ-de-Mars, he had never felt so well at his ease.

II

Growing up on his father's lands at La Ferté-Joyeuse in the Sologne, doing the things that fortunate boys do everywhere, with younger brothers to favour or shun, sisters to love and vex, birds to shoot, horses to school, catechisms and deponent verbs to commit to memory, young William Neilson had small curiosity about his parents' world. He knew that there was a house at Paris, rue Varenne, which never failed to haul a cloud into the room. The lad wondered why, having one house, or rather castle, they should require another.

One day, by an inadvertence of his mother, he had a subject to inhabit it: Mme Duclos. A little later, he heard Mme Neilson say: "Why in heaven does the Duclos need a great hôtel in the faubourg? She never goes out, keeps no carriage, receives no calls, sees nobody but her savages." Young William began to be curious of Mme Duclos.

Riding out alone with his father, young William learned more. His grandmother, old Mme Neilson, before his father's birth, had taken as her legal child a foundling of the Hôtel-Dieu of Orléans named Marie-Ange de la Contrition. His father and the orphan had grown up as brother and sister. The sister was now widowed. Her husband, Colonel Jean Duclos, having survived with honour the war in Canada, had fallen at Yorktown in the government of Virginia in the year 1781 while detached to the staff of General Washington of the Continental Army.

In the vacation of his school at La Brienne in the county of Champagne, young William's picture of the widow gained pencil-strokes and shading. At old Mme Neilson's death in 1769, Mme Duclos had taken as her inheritance the family's particular hôtel, rue Varenne. Whether because his mother thought that saucy or that a found child was no kindred for a born Montmorency – Who knows what stains of sin or mental or physical infirmity she had brought into ancient houses! – William sensed that the ladies were not friends. Such adult discord is painful to youth. William was too young to know that women rarely blaze away at other women in snowy forest clearings, as is the masculine practice, but slash with smiles and compliments in temperate withdrawing-rooms.

In calling on Mme Duclos soon after his promotion to the Military College at Paris, William knew that he was pleasing his father, his mother something less. Fearing he might become a *casus belli muliebris*, or occasion of feminine war, the lad all but turned about at the gate. Curiosity gained the upper hand. The sensation gave way to that of disappointment when, as he stood at the alert by an English cannon in the court, the foot-man brought him a note. The letter said, amid many caresses, that before she had the delight of receiving her nephew, Mme Duclos would first ask leave of his mother. Had the foot-man been other than an armed American of six feet in height, young William might have sworn a gentleman-cadet's oath.

Permission was granted (with what muffled violences, only a woman would know) and the visit proceeded. Mme Dalouhe had left the house to bully her youngest daughter, and the supper was head-to-head.

Mme Duclos spoke with frankness. Events that in the bosom of his family had been told in such-and-such a way, or told not at all, appeared to William in a blaze of American light. He had never imagined such a history. As conceited a young man as ever lived, William Neilson was not used to persons cleverer than he was, except, on certain days, M. Buonaparte. In that long evening, William learned more than in all his fifteen years.

He had the impression that nothing Aunt Duclos was saying to him had she said before or would she say again. He wondered if that were a flattery of his aunt's or an amiable habit of women in general. He resolved to adopt it.

The lady's late husband, M. Jean Duclos, while but a common soldier in Canada in the Seven Years' War, had rebelled against the surrender of the colony to the English and, by his own exertions, in the winter of the year 1760, brought ninety soldiers of the army, and a further thirty-six Canadian militia, Acadians and native men, women and children across the sea to Rochelle.

In the shame of loss and defeat, such an instance of French obstinacy soothed the injured pride of the public and was brought to the attention of His Christian Majesty, who rewarded M. Duclos with a commission and the ribbon of the Order of Saint-Louis.

King Louis, the fifteenth ruler of that name, wishing to hear no aspersions on the conduct of the army commanders, the marquis de Montcalm, the chevalier de Lévis and General Neilson, thought better to punish the administration of the Intendant of Canada, M. Bigot. The process spun out over two years. In reality, the bankrupt Court sought every pretext not to pay the King's war-time debts to the poor Canadians. The extortions of M. Bigot and his friends were so flagrant that every obligation must be examined or *visée* and, if found fraudulent, stricken from the record.

"The poor *habitants*, who had given their all to preserve the colony for France, were turned out as beggars."

The departure of the French governor and military officers from Canada in 1760 had left behind a land burned to ashes, and, tottering above the ruins, a tower of playing-cards. Since there was never a paper-mill in New France, but always a long dark winter with nothing for an unlettered population to do but play at cards, those items, once retired from play and signed on the back by Governor General Vaudreuil and M. Bigot, or a creditable merchant, had for years served as the circulating currency. Super-added to the cards were innumerable receipts, ordinances and bills, issued during the seven years of war under the signs-manual of M. Montcalm and Mr Neilson, for supplies, wages and freights for the army and presents for our native allies. All were obligations of the King of France and might be sold and bought, for the debts retained a spectral value in commerce of two sols per livre; or, as we say in affairs, were priced at a discount of 90 per cent; or, as gamesters have it, offered a 10-to-1 chance against being honoured.

"The Kings of France have ever been indifferent debtors, nephew."

Those cards and ordinances General Neilson's widow engaged to pay at sight, in specie and in full. She instructed M. Le Ber, banker at Mont-Réal, to call in and pay in Spanish silver the whole amount for which she would supply bills on Quito and Mexico. She said she had given her word to her late husband.

In France, such vidual fidelity was thought an affectation and, to a certain degree, an insult to the Crown or, as we say, *lèse-majesté*. Mme Neilson had been rich but how the devil was she going to find one hundred millions in silver? True, she had sold her jewels, carried in a coach with a false floor by our William's father to Geneva, where the stones were detached and scattered into Poland, Hungary and Russia. True, the Venetian pictures had gone to England, where they occasioned that struggle of liberality such as erupts sometimes amid the well-to-do. His Grace of Devonshire wrote to say that he would be happy, even prefer, that the Titians remain at La Ferté for as long as Mme Neilson felt convenient. Milord Pembroke sent a copy of the Reni Venus, by Mr Gainsborough, as a memento of Mme Neilson's sacrifice.

Men computed that jewels and pictures, together, had brought in twenty millions. The library was sold to the King for two million francs. The two large dwelling-houses might bring another five. The farms, canal and improved lands each side of the waterway a further six or seven. Was Mme Neilson so deranged with grief for her husband that she should destroy her fortune and succession for a few starving Canadian farmers and savages who were now subjects of King George of Great Britain, and good riddance to the pack of 'em? Who cared for M. Voltaire's *arpents de neige*, or acres of snow?

"It was my maman's penance."

"Penance for what fault, aunt? From all I have been told, my grandmother was the very best of women."

"I do not know, nephew."

Then the Supernatural intervened. Or was it that miracle

of the commercial age, which is the propensity of all but a very few men and women to seek to better their conditions with the minimum of toil?

In the merchant quarter of London, known as the City, men wondered if the Widow Neilson knew something they did not know. Had the lady some intimation, from her friend the Pompadour, that at the Peace the King of France would engage to redeem the Canada Paper? Was Mme Neilson, in preserving her spotless credit, laying the foundation of a second fortune? Knowing nobody at Mont-Réal, the stock-jobbers sent their orders to the English military governor, Mr Murray, and anybody else with whom they could scrape acquaintance.

English officers beat on hanging doors and unglazed windows, begging and threatening the *habitants* to bring out their receipts. Mr Murray pasted notices on burned and broken walls that the King of France had betrayed his former subjects and the play-cards were worthless, but raked in for himself some quartermaster bills as private speculation. M. Le Ber was buying for his own as well as Mme Neilson's account. The discount fell to 70 per cent and then to 56 per cent. Those who had bought in early – and all boasted to have done so – had quadrupled their money in half a year.

Captains brought back to London bales of the debt-paper in ballast, which tripped up the waiters in the coffee-places in 'Change Alley and made crazy heaps in the counting-houses of Lombard-Street. M. Le Ber wrote to Mme Neilson from

Mont-Réal that, such was the speculative fever in town, even card-money had become unfindable. The *Journal de La Haye* reported from Paris that the French Court was at that moment preparing a scheme of redemption for the Canadian bills.

That was not true but, as it were, made itself true. The new Secretary of the Marine, M le duc de Choiseul, disliked his forerunner and thought the Canadian bankruptcy quite as shameful as the terms of the capitulation at Mont-Réal. More to the matter, the unpaid Canadian debts were destroying the King's credit. A statesman of ability and experience, M. de Choiseul knew the only certain truth of diplomacy, which is to give gracefully what you can no longer afford to with-hold.

"I heard that M. le duc hated my maman, and not only for forcing the King's hand. He hated her because she was a woman who had engaged in affairs of the Treasury. I think he found that a deformity of the natural order."

Men of the Finance were brought to the Palace of Versailles with the single instruction that Mme Neilson should be excluded, by name, from the liquidation. No bills, receipts, promises-to-pay or card-money from Mme Neilson or her agents might, on any presumption, be received into the composition. Those with long memories reminded M. le duc de Choiseul that, during the vacancy in the île de France in 1730, Mme Neilson had, without authority or even informing the Court, allotted the King's lands *gratis* to freed blacks. The Widow Neilson was a stiff-necked woman, proud, excessively clever, far too rich for a female, insubordinate and a thorough nuisance. A couple of winters in the Castle of the Bastille at Paris would remind the lady of her duty.

"My maman had long been prepared. I begged to be allowed to share her imprisonment, but she said my first care must be my husband and, after that, my brother and, if anything of me remained, what was left of the property. Mme Dalouhe, or Marrin as she was called until marriage, proposed that she and she alone should attend her mistress in the dungeon. Marrin said she had always wished to see Paris, and was well accustomed to icy fortresses. They should ask for M. Neilson's old apartment. My maman accepted.

"We waited, dressed and ready and all boxes packed, for the exempt and his troop to come up. Days passed and then weeks. M. Duclos wrote from camp at Charenton that the place of confinement was by no means settled, and word was that my maman would be taken to the fortress of Pierre-Ancise at Lyon. He had sent his people into the inns and markets of the faubourg Saint-Antoine and found much sympathy for Maman. Best keep the lady as far as possible from the insurrectionary capital.

"Later we heard that Mme la marquise de Pompadour had reminded His Majesty of General Neilson's service in New France and of the two vessels, the *Dromadaire* and the *Junon*, that Mme Neilson had armed at her own cost and sent to Québec for the relief of Canada. Mme de Pompadour said it was His Majesty's sacred right to imprison his principal creditor, in the manner of Edward of England and Philip the Fair, but such an edict might not encourage others to open their purses. The sealed letters remained sealed, suspended like a sword above our heads."

In reality, Mme Neilson had no intention of seeking payment from the King, which was, anyway, to be not in cash but in annuities of scarcely sounder credit.

"For three days and nights beside the guard-house on the terrace at La Ferté, the Canada paper burned, brought up on tumbrils by the native men, while my maman, leaning on the cane she had started to use, stared into the flames.

"The native men had the custom of addressing my maman through an orator, La Tortue. Your father led him by the hand. M. La Tortue said:

"'*C'est assey, Djann*.' You have done more than enough, Jeanne.

"Maman nodded, and went into the house. In effect, she had done the King a service. By destroying her thirty millions in paper, she left a remainder of seventy, which reduced by half in the Visa left the King with just thirty-five millions to pay. The stock-jobbers in London roared and bellowed, but they had a pretty gain and everybody knew that. I imagine my maman was much toasted in Poultry and Corn-Hill. And they, too, I mean the English stock-jobbers, had done France a kindness. For though they had no thought for His Majesty or the poor Canadians but pursued only their own self-interest and delight in profit, yet they had obliged the Court to act with justice or, at the least, attend to the King's credit."

"You are well instructed about Canada, aunt."

"I was in the colony for two years and two months."

"With M. Duclos?"

"I was under his orders as a common soldier."

Young William could but gape.

At last, he said: "You were at Carillon, aunt?"

"Yes, nephew."

"And in the fight before Québec?"

"Yes, nephew. Both of the battles on the Plains of Abraham."

When the Americans came in to draw the curtains on the windy night, they stayed, standing against the wall.

"May I ask why, aunt?"

"My maman wished me to be Queen of Poland and Lithuania. I wished to marry M. Duclos and did so before embarking for Canada at Bordeaux."

William thought it better to hold his tongue.

"I will answer to God for the men I killed, except one."

William said nothing.

"M. de Luynes."

"What, aunt! Who brought one of the suits-at-law against your inheritance!"

Young William had done some reading.

"No. His uncle."

"M. le cómte de Luynes!"

"The same. He is dead. I shot him."

There was a murmur from the foot-men. Mme Duclos listened with attention to a foreign tongue and nodded.

"Dear friend, my companions have reminded me that M. Duclos also discharged his musket. So that he might share the odium of the murder."

"But why did you kill him, aunt?"

"He stabbed General Neilson in the dark in the place d'Armes of Québec."

"Aunt!"

"When I saw Mr Neilson bleeding in the snow, I discharged my arm without reflection. I am glad."

General Neilson had lived for another nine months. During his convalescence, he had written for Mme Neilson an account in English of his life. When, in June of that fatal year 'Fifty-nine, the English fleet appeared in the Saint-Laurent river, he placed the manuscript for safe keeping with the Ursuline Sisters of Québec. At his death, the good sisters made a copy which was, in itself, a penance and must have required many more for it was not composed for the edification of saintly women. Alas, the version entrusted to Captain Knowles of the *Auguste* was lost when that vessel, with the flower of French Canada, wrecked off the île Royale. Sometime later, by way of Captain Neiret of the *Fulgurante*, Mme Duclos received from the good sisters a second copy and, delaying only to write an account in English of the hero's death, presented it to her godmother. Mme Neilson could not at first open it but then, with an effort of her famous will, read it through at a single sitting. She asked that it not be exposed to other eyes until all those mentioned in it had gone to God.

"When I am no more, dear friend, and your father, which God postpone, it is for you to decide the fate of the memoir."

From across the quiet district, the clock of the Abbey of Saint-Germain-des-Prés struck three times.

"My Lord, I have kept you, nephew. At what hour does the gate of the College close?"

"It is always locked, aunt."

"Your mama! How shall she forgive me!"

"Have no fear, aunt. I would be no sort of soldier if I could not enter a guarded place through a weakness in the defences."

Snug in his cot as the Diane sounded from the court below, and from two feet away M. Buonaparte murmured to his nurse in Corsican, William saw that his mother, as always, had been right. William was in love: in love with his aunt and with women in general. Mme Duclos must have descried as much for, in a note that morning to thank him for his visit, she said that at the next, if it pleased him, he might bring a companion. That companion, as my reader may remember, was M. Buonaparte in the passage at the opening of this volume, placed there not in its temporal order, but in homage to its historical character.

William was elated. He had carried the loss of Canada with him since his earliest childhood, like the weakness of an artery, or a deformity of speech. It had leered at him in the schoolroom at La Brienne. How often he had said to himself that his grandfather's force, of just five hundred men, was too weak to cover every landing-place upstream of Québec. Had General Neilson not been killed, he yet might have fallen on the English rear and provoked a sally from inside the city. Or . . . or . . . William was too young to understand that a man has but to live for to fail. Had General Neilson died in the fights at Gingee in India, or Astarabad in Persia, or at Carillon, where he and the native men had turned the tide of battle, he might have been celebrated as the luckiest officer ever to have worn His Christian Majesty's uniform. General Neilson died, as we all must, in torment, shame and defeat.

But yet, and before his eyes, Aunt Duclos had pulled a scorched standard from the blaze.

William did not speak of what Mme Duclos had told him, not to M. di Buonaparte, nor even to his father. He thought it not wise of his aunt to have spoken so, but also not wicked, for he believed that she had no intention of placing a secret or division between him and his mother. He understood, with a start of novelty, that Mme Duclos was not a saint but a woman, who had no child and had lost the husband she had loved and admired above all people on earth. It was as if she needed to have another take up some of the weight of her history. Having reasoned thus, William lost some of his distress for it was a task to which he felt equal.

III

There are traces of vanity in many virtuous actions and young William Neilson knew, even at nine years old as he stepped towards the ring of boys shrieking *Nabulio! Nabulio!*, that his motives were not Christian. It was recreation in the icy exercise-yard of the school of La Brienne in the county of Champagne, *anno* 1779. There were other of the King's scholars no more fortunate than M. Buonaparte, military orphans and sons of landless barons who had stepped down from farm-carts in clogs and woollen bonnets, or giants from Martinique as black as pitch, but none was sallow and greasy of complexion, maladroit, with hair to the four winds and a nose like Polichinelle, and all were named after saints and could muster at least one sentence of intelligible French.

The circle of boys opened to admit William, but he passed through and took his stance by the blazing islander. William was no puny outcast like M. Buonaparte. William felt not so much superior to his fellows but, for reasons he could not unravel, at a tangent to them. Young as he was, he had an idea that good is rarely found in crowds. Meanwhile, the alteration in the balance of force took the charm out of the torture and the boys drifted away.

The reverend fathers (of the Minime order) were relieved that the little Corsican had for protector a lad who, though one year younger, was the son and grandson of major generals. The boys' friendship became as unalterable as the Mass. A year passed, and then another, and the friends began to draw away from their fellows, William in Latin, French and German, M. Buonaparte in mathematics, geography and ancient history. It was as if the other lads were bogged in the fathomless mud of Champagne.

To solicit a place for a younger brother, young Buonaparte's parents visited the school. They were dressed rather for the Palace of Versailles than for a country convent in the February fog. M. Carlo di Buonaparte affected the coolness of a great gentleman, from under which a Mediterranean warmth seeped out like steam from a dented kettle. Mme di Buonaparte was pretty and, in the way of such things, gave her son a touch of prestige. Had William but known it, the Buonapartes' only luxury was lawsuits.

William, young M. Buonaparte and two others were selected for the École militaire. They set off for Paris in October 1784, marshalled by the reverend principal, in two respectable coaches. At Nogent-on-the-Seine, the scholars transferred to a water-coach and came into Paris as night was coming down on the third day. They disembarked at the port Saint-Paul.

The Royal Military College of Paris was accommodated in a building that like many of the age of King Louis XV seemed designed as much for beauty as for the conduct of business. It stood on the south side of the Champ-de-Mars, just to the west of the famous veterans' hospital established by Louis the Great, the hôtel des Invalides. Begun in the 'Fifties under the impulsion of the maréchal de Saxe, and placed on strong financial legs by Mme de Pompadour and the banker Pâris-Duverney, the school could call on two millions each year to lavish on the formation and comforts of four hundred young gentlemen. Thus the soldiers of His Christian Majesty were caressed in the Paris suburbs at each end of their service, while the service, I suppose, took care of itself.

The condition of entry into the academy was not valour, nor mental ability nor strength of body, but four degrees of patrilineal nobility. There were questions over the descent of both our lads.

The Buonaparte had the friendship of the military governor of the island of Corsica, M. de Marbeuf, and that was worth an infinity of quarterings.

In the matter of young William, the Department of War wrote into Scotland. The chief herald of that kingdom, the Lord Lyon, sent from Edinburgh by express a vellum parchment of three feet in breadth and four in depth. The document was written in Minuscule Scottish Secretary, a hand that not the hereditary Judge of Arms, nor the Genealogists of the King's Orders, nor the Cabinet of Titles, nor the faculty of the University of Paris was able to read. Attached was a seven-generation pedigree, depicted as an inverted pyramid, with here and there such devices as a blinded owl and a stricken walrus *gardant*. Acclimated to that sort of thing by the tutors of the Irish cadet-candidates, the Department of War admitted our scholar. William was lodged in a cell on the topmost floor, with M. Buonaparte his chum. A single window looked down on the parade court.

The dusty scamps were, of a sudden, toy seigneurs. They were robed in blue justaucorps and scarlet breeches and topped off with hats trimmed with silver. They were fed to the neck and drank wine at table. The two friends read like oxen: M. Buonaparte Plutarch in translation and M. Rousseau, William Mr Hume, Principal Robertson and Dr Adam Smith. They reasoned in a style and language that would have distressed the good fathers at La Brienne.

William learned to fence with a minimum of movement, his point always directed at his adversary's chest; to achieve on an intact horse without recourse to the whip the equitation exercises called *piaffe* and *passage*; and to dance the minuet as neatly as a lady. In their recreations, the boys tussled on the green beyond the school, known as the plain of Grenelle, or William read to his friend from Mr Boswell's

History of Corsica. (For all his passion for England, as the refuge of General Paoli and friend to Corsican independence, M. Buonaparte knew not a word of English.)

M. Buonaparte was no longer the butt of puerile taunts as at La Brienne. The paying pupils regarded him, as all the King's scholars, and all those destined for the *savant* or technical branches such as the engineers and artillery, with a tint of compassion. In a class of fifty in mathematics, only William and M. Buonaparte paid attention. M. Buonaparte returned slights now not with his feet and fists but with an hauteur that William sought, with care, to modify. They had reached that stage in the companionship of school where oddity might be tolerated or even cherished; but M. Buonaparte's ardour for Great Britain, his contempt for France, and his crazy orthography were not appreciated. The Corsican, in his turn, detested his fellows' nonchalance and their Theban love affairs.

On Sunday after chapel, the lads conducted firing exercises and manoeuvres on the Champ-de-Mars. Parents and tutors were invited to attend. William's father was always present and did not fail to speak to the pupils destined for the artillery service. What hurt M. Buonaparte, as William could see much better than anybody, was the sight of young Mme Neilson descending in billows of Indian taffeta from a coach-and-six. Signor Carlo di Buonaparte was in poor health, and had been ruined in both fortune and constitution by a project to drain an unwholesome marsh on the limits of the town of Ajaccio and plant it through with mulberry trees. William wondered if His Majesty might have been better advised not to entertain the cadets like princes, but have them live on munition-bread and well-water like the soldiers they were destined to direct. The magnificence of their existence must, in the end, William thought, place a gulf between the poor scholar and his family.

M. Buonaparte knew nobody in Paris, and had not money to make excursions into town, licit or illicit. A visit to William's parents in the rue Saint-Honoré was unsuccessful. The talk was of the Court and M. Buonaparte was stiff and morose. Only Mme Duclos could calm the angry insular. To assuage his homesickness, she made him raviolis with her own hands. Sometimes, but not often, they spoke all in Italian.

Ill fortune struck in February 1785. Word came that Signor Carlo di Buonaparte had succumbed at Aix-en-Provence to his illness. His elder son was now in charge of a poor and numerous family. M. di Buonaparte could no longer afford to dawdle at the college. He must pass out officer that year. To achieve that, he must be examined not only in the first volume of Bezout's *Cours de mathématiques*, but in the three succeeding for which it was the usual practice to read for a second year.

M. Buonaparte set up head-quarters in the college library. Walled in by books, he ceased to attend the rue Varenne. At the examinations in August, our scholar obtained the grade of forty-two out of the fifty-eight successful candidates. Only William recognised his friend's achievement. On September

1st of that year, M. Napoléon de Buonaparte was appointed sub-lieutenant in the company of bombardiers of the regiment of La Fère. If Marshal Neilson had a part in that commission, neither that officer nor M. Buonaparte said so. William, now sergeant-major of one of the four cadet-divisions, was to remain another year until he was sixteen and a half.

M. de Buonaparte left for the regiment, then at Valence in the Dauphiné, towards the end of October 1785, but not before he had discharged his final duty.

In relations of friendship, as on many farms and country estates, there are dismal or marshy tracts where it is unwise or tedious for the house or strangers to step. None the less, M. de Buonaparte did so.

They were rambling in the plain of Grenelle, talking of Canada.

M. de Buonaparte said: "I concede, Neilson, that your grandfather was a brave man, and a capable leader of savages, but he was quite unschooled. A trained officer would have seen that the English preparations at cap Rouge were a feint to disguise the descent at Anse-au-Foulon. More even than the booby Montcalm, or the thief Bigot, General Neilson lost Canada."

William was bowled over.

After a time, William said: "All that is subject to dispute, Buonaparte, and, centuries from now, shall feed the quarrels of military philosophers. What is not in dispute is your intention in speaking so to me. M. de Buonaparte, you can have had no purpose in doing so but to annul our friendship."

"Not at all, Neilson. Your view of military affairs is clouded by the prejudices of your rank. You are scarce different from those fellows at College whose only exertion in life will have been to be born. If you wish to advance in the service, you must see the world as it is."

"No doubt, M. Buonaparte, but that is true equally of you and of all men and women under heaven. All that remains is your ill-will towards me. I wish you well, Lieutenant Buonaparte."

They set off through the fields in opposed directions.

William could not, for an instant, have suspected that as his friend embarked on the military career, Napoléon Buonaparte wanted no souvenir of either his enemies or his single friend.

IV

As sometimes happens at such youthful partings, William felt both bereft and liberated. The solitude and monotony of his Sunday visits to the rue Varenne delighted him. Selfish youth, he wished the house always to be the same.

"Are you displeased with me, nephew?"

"No, Aunt Duclos, how could I be?"

"Forgive me, but I believe you are." Mme Duclos was

smiling. "Now, young friend, what was out of shape this evening so as to disturb that good nature we have learned to love and, to a degree, expect? Was it your supper, or your wine, my talk, or my toilette? Or the railleries of Mme Dalouhe?"

"No, my lady. All were perfection."

Mme Dalouhe spoke. "He's jealous, the little rat."

"What can you mean, Mme Dalouhe?"

"You had a visit. That's what stuck in his arse."

An English gentleman, Mr Stokes, had been in the saloon when William arrived, stayed a quarter-hour, and left, but not before giving the boy his card.

"The English gentleman was charming. He speaks French of greater purity than ever did Father Massillon."

"Mr Stokes is a gallant officer who did us a great kindness in Canada: on the Plains of Abraham and later at the île Sainte-Hélène by Mont-Réal. I am as obliged to him as to any person on earth. He is now a civil man, and has made in trade what the English call a 'plum', and we French a great estate. He is a widower. I am a widow. He is English. I am French. He is a man. I am a woman. He believes that we might combine without redundancy."

William, hitherto merely sulky, was in despair.

Mme Duclos had pity on him. She said: "Dear Mr William, I gave my heart to M. Duclos to keep."

In the egoism of youth, William had no thought for the parting visitor. He could not imagine the condition of an

Englishman's heart. He did not know that, placed within that British organ, as in a sort of chapel, were two pictures that had sustained its owner through his widowhood. The first was of Mme Duclos, her long hair falling down her common soldier's tunic, kneeling beside the dying General Neilson on the battle field of the Plains of Abraham. The second was that same woman-soldier, at the capitulation on the île Sainte-Hélène, seated, in that same dirty tunic, while the native captains gave their counsel and General Amherst stamped like a warhorse at the sound of the trumpet. William could not have imagined that Captain Stokes, as he descended the perron of the hôtel, with one of those very Hurons now much advanced in years, said out loud in his native English: "So that is that."

Captain Stokes had seen enough of women in his seven-and-forty years to know that, where love is not returned, no campaign of sighs, glances into the far distance, lines from Klopstock or Shakespeare, letters from remote places or unconsidered actions will kindle love in the lady, but rather render their originator wearisome. Any imputation, even by accident, of some fault of heart on the feminine side will make its source absolutely hateful. Mr Stokes resolved to cherish the memory of his wife and tend his daughters; also, with diminished enthusiasm, their husbands and children.

In that spirit of virile resignation, Captain Stokes gave the Huron a golden guinea, which was refused as not being money of the country. Opening his purse, Mr Stokes exposed its contents. The Canadian took out two sols, the tax in double by reason of the imposture.

"I'll lay nines she do marry."

"Please, Mme Dalouhe, do not encourage a young officer to game."

William Neilson forsook play but, for a gentleman-cadet of the Royal Military College in the city of Paris, there are more profound temptations.

V

No longer constrained by M. Buonaparte's pride and poverty, William Neilson absconded to attend the theatre of the Porte Saint-Martin. One night during the Carneval, behind the scene in the last act of *Alceste*, an opera dancer brushed against him, and Gentleman-cadet Neilson fell out of the world. He forgot his mother and his father, brothers and sisters, woods, rivers, fields and ponds, College, friends, King, honour, profession, the land of France and the house in the rue Varenne. The world had contracted to the top of Mlle Suzanne Pluchart's legs. When the lad woke two months later, Mlle Pluchart had departed with her carriages and horses, securities, jewels, furs and gowns, and the bills he had given for those luxuries were coming back at him.

"William. It is you. What a pleasure that you have come."
Mme Duclos had that look of having woken from a dream.

"Little runt's left his balls somewhere."

"Please, dear friend."

Mme Duclos walked to her writing-desk, dipped a pen in
ink and wrote something. She brought it over to William.

"As you see, nephew, it is in blank."

William's shame was such that taking his aunt's bill added
scarcely a jot to it.

"I shall not inform my brother of this gift for a reason I
shall now state. I have made you sole heir to the chief part of
my property, such as it is. It is your money, not mine, that you
are spending, M. Croesus."

"I love you, Aunt Duclos."

"And I love you, Nephew Neilson. And so, in her own
fashion, does Mme Dalouhe."

"Piss!"

William no longer attended the salle de la Porte
Saint-Martin.

VI

The Sunday next after that distressful incident, William
was summoned to the rue Varenne to assist his aunt with
an American visitor whom she suspected of being unschooled

in the French language. Mme Dalouhe was in the anti-chamber.

"Come to gawp at Auntie's titties, have we?"

"With a side-glance, Mme Dalouhe, at your own magnificent chest."

"Oo-oo-oo."

Mme Dalouhe was delighted to have return of fire. She looked at young William as if to say: Just you wait till I've brought up my Coehorn mortars.

William came into a group of gentleman talking in English about the poet Shenstone. He was presented to a sailing-man from Massachusetts, Captain Sloat, who stood as if he had not so much dressed as had himself bound in cloths. Mme Duclos entered and offered the American gentleman her hand.

"My! Ma'am, you've brushed up a spot since last I had the honour."

Mme Duclos smiled. "While you, Mr Sloat, have lost none of your New England candour."

That was pitched too far a-beam of the whaling-man.

Young William said: "I believe, Captain Sloat, that Mrs Duclos does not wish to spin old yarn."

"Well, the lady's the boss."

"Gentlemen, I was once under the orders of Captain Sloat and I would not hesitate to be so again. But here, in my house, and on land, I am," and Mme Duclos paused to savour the word, "the boss." She spoke English, like William's father, with a Scotch tone. (William's mother disapproved of foreign languages, except a very little Italian.) "Let us go into the garden, so you may smoke, Mr Sloat, if you please. My godfather, General Neilson, was especially fond of tobacco."

After supper, William was deputed to light the mariner to his lodging. As they came out into the rue Varenne, Mr Sloat seemed to grow in each dimension. His paces lengthened and his hips swung. He pulled off his tie and unbuttoned his coat.

"Where d'ye find an honest drink in this famous city of Paris?"

It seemed that Champagne, for Mr Sloat, too much resembled branch-water.

"I shall show you, Captain Sloat, so long as you say what you intended to say to my aunt."

"Depends on the establishment. And the company. And the drink."

"Do not fear, Mr Sloat."

The pair crossed the river to Les Halles to a street that was out-of-bounds to the gentleman-cadets and, for that reason and no other, much by them frequented. At the sign of the Fosse-aux-Lions, William ordered aguardiente and lemons. Mr Sloat looked round him at the sharpers, cutthroats and idle women, and appeared satisfied.

"Not bad for a land-lubberer."

"Take your time, Mr Sloat."

Captain Sloat lit a pipe and began.

"Back in 'Sixty, in the fall, I was returned from the Banks with oil when I was called in to Boston by my owners, Rankin and Cleary. In the parlour, I found Mr Rankin shut up tight with another gentleman and an Indian. Mr Rankin asked if *Ichabod* was sound and rigged and I said she was. He said I was to be under the orders of Mr Duclos, which was the other gentleman.

" 'Monsieur Sloat,' said the gentleman in a Frenchish way, 'the cargo is not oil.'

" 'I figured as much,' I said.

"So I went up to Nantucket and dried out my people and set them to stores and rigging. Mr Duclos landed with his Indian and we put up sail and coasted up in squalls. At Arundel, we came into a bank of fog. We reefed in and went on, dead slow, dropping the lead every quarter-hour. Above the fog, the tops of broken firs poked out like the spears of the Devil's army. The Indian stood on the sprit, turning his head from side to side, I guess looking for something that Indians can see and we folks cain't. We saw not a dead soul. If there was a farm, it had been abandoned or burned by the French and Indians. When the light went, we put out fore-and-aft anchors. Then Duclos told me we were picking up folks not in good standing with His Majesty of Great Britain and would take them across the ocean. I had estimated that.

"The fog gave place to rain and then snow, great flakes of

the stuff that deadened every sound. Then the Indian raised his hand. Nothing more. We had the bow-gun loaded and fired two shots. That was the signal. After an age, and muffled by the snow, we heard a shot in reply and then a second.

"We dropped in a desert bay, twelve fathom, and there, standing on a shelf of rock amid the falling snow, was the prettiest lad you ever saw with a buck on his shoulders. Duclos and the Indian took the small boat. Mr Duclos splashed out while the Indian beached. I watched through my glass and saw the durn'd strangest thing. Duclos and the lad just stood there, two feet apart, looking at each other's faces. Then the boy put down the buck, reached for Duclos's hands and kissed them.

"Weel, we have that sort of thing on ship-board, in some companies more than others, and who is to tell with French bodies. The lad sure was boss, for people were running up to him and taking his orders. By now, we had the shallop down and launched and the people were lining up on the shore. Indians were putting fire to huts and tarps. One of the shallop men said there were 127 cits, a six-pound cannon and four dogs. The cannon was to show they weren't licked.

"Well, we stuffed them in some ways or other. I have seen slaves brought from Gorea in better ease. By now there was just the lad, two Indians and Duclos and the small boat. The boy had a bag-pipe with him and he climbed up on a rock and blew the saddest sound I ever heard.

"It was a lament, I think. A Scotch lament. A lament for General Neilson, who was Scotch."

"I thought the boy must be some king or prince. I am not the curious sort but, once under-way, I asked Duclos who he was. '*She*, Captain,' said Duclos. 'She is Mrs Duclos and she has brought these people out of the ship-wreck of Canada.'

"Weel, after that, I didn't ask questions. It was the very same misses who had a thousand-dollar bounty on her head. I had my cook run up something for her but maybe she don't like our chowder and biscuit, for she did not touch it. She just stood at the taffrail, hour after hour, looking into the west. She must have been talking to God, for we made the crossing in thirty-six days, just two dead, and they'd have died on shore. The tub was so low in the water that a sea-fowl a-lighting on the top-sail spar would have sunk us, but we covered a hundred mile most days."

"What pavilion did you fly?"

"Eh?"

"Your flag, Mr Sloat."

"Sometimes English, sometimes Spanish, depending on who we come up at. At the anchorage at Larochelle, Duclos left in the small boat, and he must have had heft in town, because in the bat of an eye there were wagons and teams on the dock."

He paused.

"Please continue, Mr Sloat."

"Well, I was well curious to learn more of folks who could rustle up twenty pair horses in an hour, so I set my second to command and my purser to make a cargo of French print-cloth and brandy-wine, and then we were rolling through this fine land, where there is no timber, the houses are of brick or stone and every place is cultivated . . ."

"I know France a little, Mr Sloat."

". . . till we came into a barrens of birch-trees, ling and ponds, and the cartmen sang out we would be there before the light went.

"We came on a made road, and turned between gates along a path between old trees, facing each other like sentries on guard. Ahead was the largest house I'd ever seen, higher and wider than anything on our side the water, with the sun blinding us from the windows. We crossed a bridge and were getting down when a young lad . . ."

"My father . . ."

". . . came round the angle of the house, saw us, spun about and ran back whence he'd come, shouting orders over his shoulder. The place was of a sudden like a kicked ant-hill, people crossing all over one another, carrying tables and plates and linen and great steaming kettles of vittal. Servant girls went down the line with cans of milk for the babies, bobbing up and down to the Indians. A naval man, Mr Neiret, the same who whipped the British Royal Navy on the Chesapeake, ran up and shook my hand. His lady was in back ready to pop.

"Then the lady came round the corner of the house, with a skirt maybe six yards in the round, and a black stain at the front. In the rush, she may-be knocked over a pot of ink. Behind her, Mrs Daloo was running with shawls. The men bowed, the women bobbed curtesies and the Indians raised their arms and shouted. Mr and Mrs Duclos were kneeled on the stones, heads down. I am not the kneeling sort, but I tell you, lad, that I took off my hat. And, you know, young friend, all I could hear was that damned bag-pipe from the far side of the ocean."

Captain Sloat was weeping.

"Take your time, Mr Sloat."

"The lady came up, tried to raise Mrs Duclos, but she would not budge, her tears splashing off the stones. Then Mrs Duclos looked up, her face shining with tears, and showed something in her hand. It was a hand-kerchief all red from dried blood.

"The lady stepped back as if she had been knocked in the face. Then she gathered herself and said in English: 'Mr Duclos, kindly present me to this gallant officer.'

"Then she turned, and said aloud in French, with Duclos whispering in English to me: 'There shall be long time to grieve, but now we will thank God that M. and Mme Duclos are brought safe over the water. Mme Duclos, will you take your brother and M. Neiret at that end of the table? M. Duclos and Captain Sloat, will you be kind enough to sit with me?'

Here the lady lifted her voice. 'You Canadians and soldiers of the King, know that the friends of Mr and Mrs Duclos are my friends. Sit where it pleases you. May I suggest you eat and drink in moderation, for you have been through hard going.' Then she sat down. That lady was one gristly squawse."

"Mr Sloat, you are speaking of my late grandmother!"

"Beg pardon. The lady turned to me and said in English she would pay the freight and insurance for both crossings, and also supply the return cargo. I mumbled something but Mrs Duclos came up, with one of the squawses, and the lady sprang up, and ran with them to the house, crying: 'Attend to Mr Neiret!'

"Neiret! Who broke the English line in the Chesapeake was shaking like a poplar in a gale. Your father tried to hold him, but he brushed free and made to draw sword. The Indians tied and gagged him and brought him to us and we filled him with brandy and threats. There is a kind of bridge . . ."

"Mr Sloat, I was born in that house."

". . . and all the people, farmers and working folks, were gathered there and chittering, and Duclos told me what they were saying: Mr Neilson is fallen in battle. Miss Joyous and Mr Duclos are married. Mrs Neiret is in her labours. More had happened that day than in a hundred years. Then a window flew up, and Goodie Daloo was shouting like a market-wife:

"'Captain Neiret! God has given you two sons.'

"And we were gathered round Mr Neiret, punching him and shaking his hand, while he was blushing like an old maid."

Mr Sloat was weeping again.

"Then there was a cannon shot, and another. Mr Daloo and your father had rigged up the cannon brought from Canada. I thought, I thought, that the old world is dead but, at the same time, something fresh and new was being born. The Indians had lit fires on the stones and were dancing and shouting. In front of the house there are two long buildings . . ."

William did not interrupt.

". . . each one of which would house a warship's company. The women were put in the riding-school and the men in the tennis, while the Indians bunked in their cloaks by their fires. I was put up in the house, the walls of the room top to bottom hung with paintings of bare titties. I never saw so much open tit outside of New Orleans."

William thought that a just, even precise, description of Reni of Bologna's *Toilet of Venus* and Titian's *Judgement of Paris*, both now in England.

"Next day, Mrs Duclos came to call on me. She was still in her damn'd uniform, the sleeves rolled to the elbow. I guess she had lain all night in it beside her mother. She said that Mrs Neilson was suffering, and could not thank me in person, but had written to my owners. With the letter were sight bills on New-York, a thousand Spanish dollars for me and another thousand for my people, and a diamond brooch for my lady, not that then I had one, but I got one damn quick just as soon as I was back in the Commonwealth. They was lined up on the dock for my refusal."

"Mme Neilson was as generous as she was brave."

"She gave me her coach and Daloo to drive it, the same who died of the shits at Valley Forge: me, John Winthrop Sloat, riding through France with four glass windows and a crown on the doors, and two men in livery up in point."

Captain Sloat was weeping pure spirit.

William stood up. He said: "Thank you, Mr Sloat, you have done me a service I shall not forget." Then, touched by something of his grandmother's magnificence, the youth said: "Will you take my purse, Mr Sloat, should you wish to make a night of it?"

"That I think I shall, young fellow."

As William crossed to the windy street-door, he saw two of the ladies slide between the tables to console the grieving sailor.

"Did you decant Mr Sloat's story?"

"It was not difficult, aunt. Three bottles of rhum and . . ."

"Enough, M. William, spare us!"

"And how many nasty women?"

"If you please, Mme Dalouhe."

"All that I shall keep locked in my heart, beside the picture of you, Aunt Duclos, and that of you, Mme Dalouhe."

"Don't you dare put me anywhere near your heart, you slug!"

VII

If young William had learned anything in his military formation, it was that defeat is a wiser master than victory. The
Peace signed at the Palace of Versailles after seven years of
war in 1763 brought with it the seeds of enlightenment. For
William and the more reflective lads at the College, it was
evident that, without a fighting navy to match that of Great
Britain, France could not defend its overseas counters and
factories and must give up any thought of a world-wide commerce; while, without a system of state finances on the English
pattern, approved and guaranteed by the public in a Parliament, she could not hope to match the military expenditure
of her island rival. The question was: How to introduce popular representation into absolute government?

The loss of Canada had other consequences. In the year
1776, with no more fear of the French to the north and west
and, more particularly, their native Canadian allies, the English in America rebelled against the masters across the sea. The
French ministers saw a chance of recovering a portion of the
prestige and territory lost on the Plains of Abraham and in
India. Although the duc de Choiseul, minister of the marine,
had made good the naval losses of the late war, France was then
not ready to test her own arms against Great Britain.

Because of his proficiency in the English language, his
unequalled experience of North American warfare, and his

mean and obscure birth, M. Duclos was the choice of all to lead a clandestine military mission to General Washington's rebel army.

When the English ambassador submitted a Note of protest, he was told that Duclos was a common volunteer of no family and less importance but with a depraved taste for American forests. As for Dalouhe or whatever-is-his-name, he was a stable-groom at some pitiable property in the Sologne. If we must debate such fellows, the French ministers said, what about the English filibustiers plaguing Saint-Domingue?

In reality, Colonel Duclos became intimate with General Washington, and remained so even after the French declaration of war and the arrival of General Rochambeau's force in 1781. Colonel Jean Duclos was killed in the fight to take Redoubt 9 at Yorktown, in the government of Virginia. He was buried beneath the rampart with his fallen men. Pierre Dalouhe died of dysentery at camp in Pennsylvania.

All that William knew, because everybody knew it. He knew nothing more and, sensible lad, applied to Mme Dalouhe. Mme Duclos had retired to her rooms, and William found his enemy in the saloon at her work by candle-light.

"What do you want, rascal?"

William brought a chair from the wall and sat down opposite the lady, not three feet distant.

William began with caution. He said: "Tell me about your life here, Mme Dalouhe."

To William's surprise, Mme Dalouhe laid down her work on her lap.

"Well, after your parents married, before you were born, we all came up here, everybody but that she-devil Mme Plaie, the old wet-nurse. We were cosy in the house, M. and Mme Duclos in the logis, Her Ladyship and us in the east wing and the wild men in the west. Her Ladyship was often sad, as she was before General Neilson came into our lives and made us all happy. There was something in his papers from Canada that broke Her Ladyship's heart, she never told me what it was. Some days, she would just sit, rocking back and forward, while Mme Duclos held her on one side and me on t'other.

"Later when I asked Mme Duclos, she said it was about some girl in Canada who had been killed, but how that was Her Ladyship's doing, how would I know. Once, I heard her cry out in her sleep: 'Adeline', I think, 'Adeline', 'Adeline'. She started going to the convent, first just for the month of Lent, and then all of Advent as well. She would not let me come to attend her."

"The convent, Mme Dalouhe?"

"Les Thelles, at Romorantin."

"What did she do there?"

"How should I know? Her Ladyship went alone by post."

Mme Dalouhe said what she did know. "In the valise, I packed one cotton dress, a cap, needles and thread, no under-linen; no powder or rouge; hemp-soled espadrilles, two pairs; soap and medicines; also money in coin.

"Then one day, in 'Sixty-three or -'four, when Her Lady-ship was here, a fat fellow came waddling over the court. His card-of-visit said he was secretary at the English Embassy. The wild men were for beating him up, but I took the card and Her Ladyship received him. He was Scotch like M. Neilson."

"Mr Hume?"

"Yes, and with him the Duke of Scotland and his brother and their mad old tutor."

William had heard that the lands of His Grace of Buc-cleuch and Queensberry were extensive, but not that they were co-terminous with the kingdom of Scotland.

"Oh, the lads were sweet. They used to hold my wool for me while the other fellows prosed away or fell over their canes like toads. The tutor-man was the most absent person in company I ever saw. He would sit for hours, staring into nothing, and chomping broken sugar in his buckle teeth. At a signal from Her Ladyship, one of the wild men would take away the bowl, fill it again with sugar and place it on his lap, without the loon noticing."

"Dr Smith has erected perhaps the most beautiful fabric of moral theory since the Sermon on the Mount."

Mme Dalouhe looked evil.

"It is philosophy, Mme Dalouhe."

"More like mouse-shit."

William wondered how two such infidels as Mr David Hume and Dr Adam Smith had made company in so orthodox a house as that of old Mme Neilson. Without being asked, Mme Dalouhe enlightened him.

"Her Ladyship had two rules for what could be said. No jacquerie—"

". . . No theme that might give vent to sentiments of Jacobitism . . ."

Mme Dalouhe ignored the intervention.

". . . and no revealing religion."

". . . nor cast any aspersion of doubt upon Revealed Religion."

Had William gone too far? Mme Dalouhe was balanced between war and peace. She came down on the side of peace.

"None of your sauce, if you please, boy."

"Certainly, Mme Dalouhe."

"The fat fellow went back to Scotland, but the lads stayed on. Then the younger one, Hugues, fell ill. We put him in the Blue chamber. Her Ladyship, Mme Duclos and I sat by him in relays day and night, while the tutor-fellow blubbered outside or walked up and down and down and up outside the saloon. The young Duke took charge and ordered the poor man to bed. Dr Quesnay came from the Palace each morning and night. The lad was bled white. I was told to give tisane, and then wine, and then tisane again. By the end, it was a relief that he should die, and suffer no more.

"The Duke took his brother's body and the half-dead tutor away. Then, a few weeks later, came a letter from Edinburgh in a sweet gold box saying that Her Ladyship had been elected to their scientific society. And then, not much later, the same without the box from the society at London; and then Berlin, Turin and Florence and who knows where? And so, in the end, the King had to forgive her for Canada and she was appointed to the French society."

"What was my grandmother's discourse to the Royal Academy of Sciences, Mme Dalouhe?"

"Is there gas?"

"Yes, we breathe it."

"I think it was about gas.

"Her Ladyship became sunnier, ceased to go to the convent except at Lent, though I know she paid the sisters' fire-wood and salt and the dowries of poor novices. Sometimes, I made her laugh.

"Then, one day in 'Sixty-nine, in December, when we were all about the fire, and Mme Duclos was reading aloud, I looked up at Her Ladyship, and she had a look that I had never seen before. Not happy, not sad, but something else that I cannot name. It was as if she had stepped out of the room and left her person behind. Mme Duclos stopped reading, stood up and closed Her Ladyship's eyes."

Mme Dalouhe was silent for a time. She said: "She was a good woman."

"She was the outstanding woman of her age, Mme Dalouhe."

Mme Dalouhe said nothing.

Fearful he might be dismissed, William said: "Tell me about M. Dalouhe."

Mme Dalouhe turned on him with something of her general savagery.

"I had to let him go."

"Of course, Mme Dalouhe."

Her face was wet with tears. "He did not go to Italy with M. Neilson, or to Canada with the Duclos. He was as good as any of them. He had a right to see the world."

"I know, Mme Dalouhe."

"And their General What's-his-name, who did not even speak French. What sort of general is it that don't speak French?"

Having studied with care General Washington's campaigns, young William thought that a venial fault.

Mme Dalouhe raised her voice. "God damn America, which killed our men: the General, M. Duclos and my poor Pierre, the handsomest man that ever walked ground; not much up top, mind, but it's not what's up top that matters to a lady, if you take my meaning."

By the favour of Mlle Pluchart, William had an idea of Mme Dalouhe's meaning.

"That man could not even write in French!"

William woke up.

"Could not my aunt translate the General's English letter for you, Mme Dalouhe?"

"I did not want to add to Her Ladyship's cares."

William saw that, in Mme Dalouhe's recollection, god-mother and god-daughter had coalesced.

"Mme Dalouhe, will you permit me to read the letter to you? I know some English."

Turning her head, Mme Dalouhe shook from her sleeve a letter with an unbroken seal. William detached the seal and read out loud, translating as best as he was able into French.

Head-Quarters, Valley Forge, Pennsylvania
March 28, 1778

Dear Mrs Dallow
It is with infinite pain that I must apprise you that your husband, Maj. Peter Dallow, died of fever in the camp of the Continental Army here at Valley Forge on the 15th inst. Col. Duclos was with him in his last hours, as was the chief surgeon of the army, Mr Otto. Mr Dallow's earthly

remains were interred that same night by the Roman rite in the yard at Norriton church. Please accept my condolences and those of my officers. I understand that Col. Duclos has written to you.

When the Army entered camp in December last, Mr Dallow was at first restricted, by the limitations placed by the French ministers, and by his unfamiliarity with our English speech, to serving Mr Duclos and the French mission. Yet in a very short time, his natural vigour, and his great ability in all matters of commissary and military transportation caused him to take a more active part in our enterprise.

At that time, the commissary's department was in desperate state, while the office of the quartermaster was labouring for want of a capable man to direct its great business. The men were on the point of mutiny. Not a hoof to slaughter and no more than twenty-five barrels of flour for twelve thousand mouths, no soap or vinegar, and men sent to farmers' houses for want of a shirt or shoes.

I had intended to throw a bridge over the Schuylkill Creek, to open supply from the farms on the north bank, but the officers in command of the works were in dispute and the work was at a stand.

When Mr Duclos informed me that Mr Dallow had never carried arms in the service of the King of France, I had no hesitation in commissioning him major in the Army, the rank unequal to his merit but for that reason less likely to breed jealousy and animosity. Mr Dallow completed the bridge in thirty hours and, at once, sent out carts to forage among the farms along the north side.

At no point did Mr Dallow apply coercive measures which, howsoever they may provide a temporary relief, cannot fail to instil fear in the people, and, even among good soldiers, a spirit of plunder and licentiousness. A week later, in an exploit that won the admiration of all my officers, he brought through the English lines two thousand blankets and as many yarn stockings made with infinite labour by the patriot ladies of Philadelphia. In my despatch to the President of the Congress on that action, I singled out your husband's uncommon exertions for praise. Mr Dallow's cheerful demeanour, admirable horsemanship and coolness under fire made him fast friends among both officers and men.

Madam, the winter-quarters of a fighting army is not a salubrious place, and we have had a hard row to hoe. By his great endeavours to ensure supply, I fear Major Dallow exposed himself too recklessly to the disease that took him from us and from you.

I can give you, madam, no consolation but that your husband died in the service of his friends. Should we, with God's help, succeed in erecting a scheme of liberty in this land, we shall remember all those who fell in that great task *and, in the first rank of them, dear madam, your brave and efficient husband.*

I have written to Mr Franklin at Paris in the matter of your widow's pension.

I am, madam, your obedient servant

G. Washington,
Commander-in-chief, Continental Army

William returned the letter.

"God bless America, Mme Dalouhe?"

Mme Dalouhe had her eyes closed. After a time, she said: "Kiss me, sweet William." And then: "Get away with you!"

As William descended the perron, he had a premonition. He raced back up the steps, praying to every saint he could think on.

He found Mme Dalouhe where he had left her, except only that the letter had fallen to the carpet. He folded it, placed it in her hands, and folded them on her lap. Her lips and open mouth were icy cold. He shut her eye-lids. His own were wet.

He wondered if he should grieve now, or later. Better later.

He ran through the rooms and beat at the door at the end.

"Aunt Duclos! Kindly come with me. It is urgent."

"You may come in, William."

He came into a tiny room, not six feet by four across, boards bare of even a drugget and the only furniture a narrow bed and a prie-dieu, at which last Mme Duclos was kneeling in her night-gown.

"I am praying, William."

"Mme Dalouhe is dead. Let me take you to her."

Mme Duclos lowered her forehead to the prie-dieu, rested a moment, and then stood up. She followed her nephew and began to run.

She said: "I came into the world with nothing and shall leave with nothing."

"I am with you always."

Mme Duclos shivered. William caught her as she fell, and held her close, as might a son his grieving mother. After a time, Mme Duclos said: "I am myself again, William."

"If you wish to return to your rooms, Aunt Duclos, I shall send a lady to attend you. I shall see to all the funeral business."

"Thank you, Nephew William."

Out in the court, William bellowed: "Wake up, you idlers. Now is the time to earn your bread for once."

Figures stirred from dark corners, doors swung open, windows rattled. In a rumble of groans and oaths, men and women shuffled in every degree of undress towards him. William said in a steady voice: "Mme Dalouhe is dead. She is in the Green Saloon. I need four gentlemen to take her to the chapel, and four ladies to make her ready there. Two ladies are to attend Mme Duclos in her bedroom. You, sir!

You are to go now to the rue des Bourdonnais and stir up M. Morel and say he is to come at once to the rue Varenne to take Mme Duclos's orders. And you, sir, are to go to Poilaine, the florist in Les Halles, with the same charge."

Those commercial addresses were not the least of the knowledge William had acquired from Mlle Pluchart.

"Do you all understand? And if I find so much as a snuffhorn missing from the house, I shall ask Mme Duclos to turn every one of you out."

Without his knowing it, a part of William's mind had continued to inquire into the decor of his aunt's bedroom. As the people went about their duties, and William kept a good eye on their hands, a finished thought came into consciousness. Aunt Duclos had not been born to riches but, on the contrary, had been a pauper. Mme Dalouhe was not her serving-maid but her equal and her friend. Aunt Duclos is strong not because she is rich but because she is poor. For only the poor can truly know the meaning of money, and work, and suffering and love and death.

William Neilson, examined on Bossut, was first in the class. He was decorated with the Order of Saint-Lazare. When his brother-cadets and his father's friends congratulated him, William attempted a manly generosity. It is not just, William said, for M. Buonaparte is by some distance the better officer. Do not be surprised (William said) if, not long from now, M. Buonaparte shall be chief citizen of a free and happy Corsica.

VIII

In the civil war of the Neilson family, my reader has hitherto seen but one camp, sat around fires, made audit of stores and munitions, walked the rounds of the pickets, supped with the common soldiers. To maintain a neutrality in the conflict, he must raise his collar, and she her hood and veil, and follow young William over the Seine river into the enemy's ground.

What is it that preserves a family in prosperity for forty generations? It was surely not that Bado de Joieus had borne Charlemagne's spurs at the Emperor's coronation in Rome for that honour had ceased to operate on the minds of men and women, except those descendants of the knight who carried the Emperor's boots. Was it God's grace, embodied in the blazon and palladium of the family, the Chalice argent, a smashed cup of old Iranian work or the Saint Grail, according to belief? Or was it, for those of a philosophical mind, a set of twists and accidents that had worked for the prosperity of the family?

Of those, it was the chance meeting of Jeanne de Joyeuse and William Neilson at the Royal Bank in Paris on December 10th, 1720 that shook the dusty standards in the chapel; and, more even than that, the small-pox that afflicted Jeanne that her lover, from knowledge he had gathered in Persia, cured. One result was that as the world began to groan and shake, one part of our family spoke English (or rather Scots), had drunk deep draughts of Scotch morals, finance and political economy and had devoted friends overseas, in Canada, the States of America and Russia. The other part cleaved to France and monarchy as the source of all distinction and its guarantor.

This division of the family was but a version, individual and yet commonplace, of what was occurring throughout Christendom and, after a delay, in the Ottoman lands, Egypt, Persia and India. It occurs to me that there is nothing unique here and that such a division of the family's forces had been executed at other cross-roads in the long history of France, and carried the Joyeuse through the Wars of Religion and the Fronde. Or perhaps it was that talisman: Sable, a Chalice argent.

Our William's father, also William (since Neilson men are William, and women Jeanne), had no faults of character but one fault of circumstance. He was born in the wrong year. Bred for a soldier's life, he had found, once he had reached military age, that one war had ended and another not yet begun. Having a bent for the artillery, he had made himself as expert as any in Europe on the casting and deployment of solid and explosive ordnance. A devotee of iron foundries and artillery ranges, he possessed an unrivalled talent for industrial organisation. He recruited the brightest men rather than the best-born. By his own efforts and, perhaps more, by attracting to his command men of technical knowledge, he had created not just the best heavy guns in

Europe but the most efficient branch of the French army. In that time, he had risen to the rank of camp-marshal without firing a shot to wound.

Marshal Neilson had inherited from old Mme Neilson a speck of that lady's pride of family and, since that pride was all but limitless, the Marshal's speck was not inconsiderable. He had married Mlle de Montmorency, who brought with her half a million francs a year in annuities on the Paris Town Hall and five millions in jewels, and became, in time, our William's mother. Since old Mme Neilson had laid waste her fortune in sending supplies to General Neilson in Canada in the Seven Years' War, and then discharging the King's debts to the Canadians, the contribution was timely. Old Mme Neilson thought her new daughter proud and so she must have been.

La Ferté-Joyeuse was (and is) a large house, and could with space to spare accommodate a score proud ladies. Mme Neilson believed that Mlle de Montmorency should have undisputed command and, since Mme Duclos would not ever again be separated from her maman, nor M. Duclos from Mme Duclos, nor the Hurons from any of the three, in the year 1763 they translated in a body to the rue Varenne. Only the malignant centenaire Mme Plaie refused to stir from her crazy cabin in the woods, but sent them on the road with rolling volleys of curses; and then, to bring bad luck to Mlle de Montmorency on her wedding-morning, died.

For some years, Mme Neilson the younger was occupied with having babies and obliterating, with indifferent success, the medieval character of her husband's country house. Yet even as she was so engaged, she nourished in her heart a small hope that over time grew large. The dukedom of Joyeuse, which had been extinguished at the sudden death of her husband's maternal grandfather, would be revived in a second creation for her husband.

For such an enterprise to please the King and his counsellors, it was necessary both that her husband gain some great distinction, but also to remove or in some way conceal the debris of her mother-in-law's irregular life. Mlle de Montmorency knew, because William had told her on making his offer of marriage, that he had been born outside the temporal bounds of matrimony, and then legitimated. She knew from the talk of the town that Mme Neilson had experimented with electricity or somesuch; and that Mme Duclos had been in Canada and done something there. For that reason, communication between the two town-houses, the one in the rue Varenne, the other new-built in the rue Saint-Honoré, was not especially brisk. With the death of old Mme Neilson in ' Sixty-nine, it ceased altogether.

Marshal Neilson understood that, at marriage, the passports of the old regime are cancelled, and application must be made in multiple copies to fine-grinding departments. He suffered agonies in being separated from his adoptive sister.

His delight knew no bounds when, in her weekly letter to her brother, Mme Duclos spoke of her friendship with young William. The gentleman-cadet, it is to be regretted, wrote to his father scarcely once in two months.

Like dismasted ships, the houses drifted apart. The mourning for Mme Dalouhe was the point of rupture. William's mother behaved with grace. Wishing to please her, and to riddle the fire, visitors to the rue Saint-Honoré told of the acres of black crêpe across the front of the hôtel Joyeuse-Neilson, the arms of the Joyeuse family above the coachmen's gate, and the stripes and stars of the American States on the flag-staff. A common servant and the famous Chalice argent of the Joyeuse! Mme Neilson replied that she had heard that Mme Dalouhe was a woman of merit and beloved of Mme Duclos.

William could not bear the flatteries. Wherever he stood in the saloon of the rue Saint-Honoré, he must betray either his mother or his aunt. He retreated to the window and looked out at the Elysian fields and the Madeleine church.

"I asked Mme Duclos to come to live with me. She has refused."

William made a half-turn. Seated near him, unattended, was a handsome woman, on the shaded side of forty years, with a freckle face unmasked by powder. She said: "I am Agnès Neiret. I knew your grandfather in Canada."

"Mme Neiret, I cannot say how delighted I am to have your acquaintance."

Something about the lady, that impression of the open air that she shared with Aunt Duclos, took away all William's reticence.

He said: "May I ask, madame: who is Adeline?"

Mme Neiret shivered. She turned to the window. There were tears in her eyes.

"She was my friend at the pension in Québec, cruelly shamed and done to death."

"By M. Luynes?"

Two young men sprang up like jacks-in-boxes, prepared, at the smallest provocation, to cut young William open.

Mme Neiret smiled through her tears, like sunshine in a shower of rain. She said: "M. Neilson, may I present my sons?"

There was a round of evil compliments. William could see that any discourse with Mme Neiret must wait.

"I see you are in the marine service, gentlemen."

They were, damn his impertinence. After another round of venomous bows, the mariners carried their unravished mother to safety. William returned to looking to the west. Yet his station, at some distance from the convivial society, seemed to attract outlaws. A burly young officer, in an exotic uniform, was examining the distant village of Chaillot. Like a stiff door-hinge after a touch of grease, William reverted to social duty.

"Sir, I believe you have but small acquaintance here."

"None at all."

"Permit me to remedy that, sir. I am Neilson, destined for the Engineers."

"Bielke, Her Majesty the Tsarina's Chevalier Guard. My father said that, at Paris, I should call on Marshal Neilson but not on Mme Duclos, who will break my heart."

"Then I shall take you only to my father. And then, if you would like, shall we sup with some of my fellows?"

The two young men marched down the saloon towards the mob about Mme Neilson. Backs formed a rampart-wall of bone and cloth, but M. Bielke battered it down.

"Mother, may I present Count Bielke of the Russian service?"

"We are not, as far as I know, at war with Her Tsarian Majesty, M. Bielke."

There was a gust of laughter.

"Mother, our families were friends in Persia."

"General Neilson saved my grandfather from decapitation, madame."

"Really, is there no place on earth where Neilsons have not performed some act of chivalry?"

A turn to her husband, who was dozing upright, took the irony from Mme Neilson's exclamation and froze the smiles on the faces of her auditors.

The lads had better fortune with Marshal Neilson.

"Oh, dear boy," he said. "Sergueï Pavlovitch came to stay with us in the provinces when I was small. How is your gallant father? Has he recovered from my sister's savagery?"

"Not at all, sir. He lives, thank God."

"William, shall you make peace between the houses in the second generation?"

"Yes, sir."

"Lieutenant Bielke: during your residence in Paris, I would wish you to treat my house as your own."

There was a commotion at the door. A naval gentleman entered, or at least the surviving parts of him. His right eye was patched, and the left sleeve of his coat was pinned to his breast. His hair was white as paper. He limped on his left leg. There were cries of pleasure and a clapping of hands. The gentleman blushed and his eyes raked the room, as if seeking reinforcement. That came in the shape of Mme Neiret and her two myrmidons. The hero looked relieved. Though eager to meet the famous Captain Neiret, William felt that his first duty was to his Russian friend.

They went, as always, to the Fosse-aux-Lions. Lieutenant Bielke had been with Souvoroff in the Caucasus. William thought: He smells of gunpowder, and we of milk.

Their guest said: "I don't like wine."

What Pavel Sergueïevitch did like was rhum mixed with apricot conserve. All agreed the drink was superior to Champagne. After a few bottles and jars, there were songs. The young Russian sang in a deep basso that drew the admiration of the whole cabaret. After a time, he proposed they go and seek a fight, which was unanimously approved as the most prosperous course of action. The alcoholic liquor, freed from its prison of glass, found much to its taste in young blood and muscle.

Having chased the Night Guard, the lads made a sortie to the English Embassy and broke many windows with stones. Finding a cabriolet, William and his new friend took on harness and hauled their companions in the direction of the river with the wise intention of depositing the vehicle in the waves. At the Butchers' Church, rue des Écrivains, looking up at the bell tower in the half-moonlight, Count Bielke said:

"Do you often climb it?"

"Once, years ago."

"I never reached the top."

There was a race to the foot of the tower. M. Bielke led the way up and was soon just a dark shape above them.

William thought: If you wish to ascend a bell-tower in darkness, dead drunk, it is wise to select a monument of the Late Gothic age. The buildings that survive of that era are embellished with every sort of decorative flourish, gargoyle, flying buttress, finial, frieze, balustrade and open-air pulpit; the which, while beautiful and edifying, offer many a precious hand- and foot-hold to the drunkard climber. On the debit side, the engineers of that age were so capable, and the wholesale butchers of Les Halles so rich, that they could raise on the marsh that is the city of Paris a bell-tower of thirty toises in elevation and nine in diameter.

William caught his breath on the sill of a tall lancet window. The wafts of rhum that had raised him sky-wards were dispersing. William looked down. His friends had long ago dropped to earth, where they were pretending to be too intoxicated to move. William's clothes were drenched with icy sweat. He was shaking fit to lose his grip on the window transom. Raising his head, he saw M. Bielke at the summit, seated beside a statue of a bull, legs over the balustrade, pipe lit, looking out over the dark city of Paris.

With his remaining presence of mind, William shouted upwards:

"M. Bielke, do you by chance have a rope about your person?"

"I am coming. Stay still."

M.Bielke came down, springing from hold to hold like a squirrel in the canopy of a wood, and came to rest just below William.

"Place your left foot on my head."

William did so.

"And drop your right foot beside it."

William did so.

"Press your face and palms against the stone."

William did so.

They descended, William's weight on his new friend's head.

William Neilson's education was complete. Mme Duclos had taught him to love. Mlle Pluchart had shown him how to be happy. Pavel Sergueïevitch had taught him to trust.

Never had the ground felt so necessary. William turned to see the archers, swelled to company strength, mistreating his companions. Count Bielke propelled him towards the officer.

"Constable, here is the leader of the miscreants. Do not spare him."

IX

William and his dismal band were released into the custody of Marshal Neilson, who neither praised nor blamed. Having no address for his Russian saviour, William called at the hôtel of the Imperial Russian Ambassador, rue Grenelle. He was perplexed to see no porter at the gate and the glass doors of the *corps-de-logis* swinging in the morning sun. Inside, colossal footmen lay face-down on side-tables or asprawl in billows of fallen window-curtains.

William found his way to M. le baron de Simoulin, in dressing-robe and night-cap, dictating to a secretary with his wig askew.

"Forgive me, Your Excellency, for intruding on your business. I was searching for my friend, Count Bielke. I am under an obligation to him."

"M. Bielke has been here. As you can see."

"Do I have your permission to inquire of your servants where he is to be found?"

"He is at Neilson's, I believe. I believe he is engaged to breakfast with Sub-lieutenant Neilson."

"Thank you, Your Excellency."

Mme Duclos's friends had a boisterous game which they liked to play on high occasions, and which they called Baggate. The goal of the exercise was to strike with a stick a rock or pave-stone so as to hit the leftward urn at the top of the perron, while the opponent party had for target the guichet in the porter's lodging. Coming into the court of the hôtel Joyeuse-Neilson, William found his Slavonian friend, sans tunic, engaged in a keening pack of Hurons in that ruinous pastime. Propped against the walls were the injured, like idols for which one has no more reverence.

"Have you sent up your card, M. Bielke?"

"No. I believed I should wait to be presented."

William was astonished by the Russian's tact.

In the saloon upstairs, Mme Duclos ran at them and took M. Bielke's hand.

"Thank Heaven that you are safe. Had you come to harm, I could not have faced your father, or Countess Lidia Petrovna."

Mme Duclos turned to her nephew. "William, it is not for me to reprimand you. I believe you have given M. Bielke an impression of yourself and of Paris that is worthy of neither. Let us not dwell on the incident."

Mme Duclos turned to William's companion.

"M. Bielke, when is your furlough expired?"

"I must leave Paris tomorrow."

"Then, will you give me the pleasure of supping with me and my nephew this evening? I shall order rooms to be prepared for you both. Then, tomorrow, my people will conduct you to the diligence."

It took a moment for M. Bielke to understand that he was under arrest. He shrugged, as men from large and wild countries are apt to do.

After supper, and after Mme Duclos had left the young men to their wine, William was summoned out into the front court. Before the steps was a carriage. Inside it was a young girl, face-down amid the cushions, sobbing. She was dressed in a cotton shift and sabots. Though he knew nothing of children, William could detect a strategy. For the child, the world was so dangerous she must always have entire dominion. William accepted that. He asked the Hurons to step back, opened the door, and sat down on the coach-step.

He said: "Young miss, the lady who will care for you was herself once an orphan like you. When she was no older than you are now, she received a stranger's kindness. Now she is old and rich, she wishes to pass that kindness to you so that you, in your turn, shall pass it to another. You will never again be hungry, or frightened, or sad, for Mme Duclos shall be hungry and frightened and sad for you. Now, young miss, sit up and we shall escort you to Mme Duclos."

The girl sat up. She seemed not so much a child as a young fox caught in a snare.

"Now place one hand on my arm, and the other on this officer's, and we shall go up to Mme Duclos. Attention! Two steps forward, and one step back . . ."

M. Bielke said: ". . . and three steps forward and two steps back . . ."

"Swing about!"

"Two steps back," the child cried, "and one in fore."

"Turn about!"

"Now! Three steps up and two steps down!"

"Four steps up and three steps down!"

"Touch your toes and turn about!"

They had reached the landing place. The lass began to tremble.

Count Bielke said: "Now tell me your name, mademoiselle, so I may announce you to Her Ladyship."

The child struggled to break free.

M. Bielke knocked on the door, opened it and bellowed:

"Her Highness the Most Transparent Princess of Brasil!"

Aunt Duclos was standing in her wrapper at the window. She turned and halted in mid-motion. William had a momentary terror for her. He feared that she might fall; or that the house would vanish, and the years with it, and Mme Duclos would stand before them in rags and scratches.

"Go, lass."

Her Royal Highness ran at Mme Duclos, who enveloped her in her arms. M. Bielke closed the door.

"A touching scene," he said.

"Will you not smoke a cigare with me in the garden, Lieutenant Bielke?"

"Please call me by name. I rather think I shall turn in. Paris is an exhausting capital."

His friend's mixture of ferocity and punctilio was very much to young William's taste.

X

William called the next day at the English Embassy. He brought with him a *posse comitatus* of glaziers, masons and plasterers. While they set up their tools and scaffolds in the front court, William was led into the Minister's cabinet. That gentleman was alone, writing at speed, his spectacles at the end of his nose. Without looking up, he said in French:

"Do you bear a grudge against me, Lieutenant Neilson?"

"No, sir, not at all. I very much regret that my brother-cadets and I supped too well. Had we come first on the

Resident of Brandenburg, or the Commander of Malta, they would have suffered from our unpardonable puerility."

"Are you sure, Lieutenant Neilson?" The gentleman stood and took off his spectacles.

"Ah, my God!"

"Please sit, M. Neilson. Or, if you would prefer, lie."

"Captain Stokes, if I had known . . . if I had suspected for an instant . . . My God!"

William groped for a chair, curled into it and put his head in his hands.

"For all my laziness and incompetence, and because I speak a few words of French, am rich and have no family or connections, His Majesty has appointed me his minister plenipotentiary at Paris and made me a knight of the realm."

"Mme Duclos did not tell me, Sir James."

"I am glad. I can bear that lady's indifference but not her stone-throwing."

"Sir, if my aunt had known that you were in Paris . . ."

". . . she would also have known that I keep my word."

Sir James Stokes was standing. On his face was a sort of inward smile. It was as if he had fallen into a habit of irony that he was no longer able to put off.

"I shall tell Mme Duclos that you are here, sir. She will be delighted that your merits, of which she has the highest appreciation, have been recognised by the ministers in London."

"A diplomatist, Mr Neilson, never tells an untruth but he

does not always volunteer a truth. Don't lie, don't tell. For your sake alone, I shall say: I did not ask to be appointed here, but I was not able to refuse with honour."

"I am sorry, sir. Also for the windows."

From beneath them, there was a sound of voices raised, and then a great smashing of glass. A second, and inimical, squad of artisans, embodied by the Secretary of the Embassy, had formed up in the court.

"It sounds like war," Sir James Stokes said.

"I shall make peace, sir."

William bowed and turned to leave.

"May I, at least, have the honour sometimes of calling on you?"

"No. It is not helpful to a young officer to frequent foreign missions."

"I regret that, sir."

At the door, William turned and said: "Forgive me, sir, if I ask what Mme Duclos did in Canada?"

Sir James Stokes turned his back and returned to his desk. He said, so quietly that William had to take a step towards him:

"The nations loved your grandfather, for they thought him one of themselves, but nothing in their world had prepared them for Mme Duclos. Nobody ever saw her in the trees; or nobody that lived to say so. As for the *habitants*, they called her the Maid of Orléans reborn who would save God's people from the English. She would have held Canada for France."

Sir James Stokes smiled at William. "That is why Mr Amherst wanted Mme Duclos hanged. And all our officers, likewise."

"Except you, sir."

Sir James returned to his writing. Do not lie. Do not tell.

Having separated the brawling glaziers, and made distribution of wages and presents, William carried his wooden throat and gypsum head back to the rue Varenne. His aunt was in the garden, unpotting flower-bulbs with her own hand. She smiled at William from under a straw hat.

"How is brave Sir James?"

William wondered if it might not be more convenient to die.

"You knew the gentleman was in Paris, aunt!"

"Of course, I knew. I am not an anchoress. And so did you, you felon."

"I did not, aunt. I swear on my honour."

"Calm yourself. My maman used to say that there are impulses of the heart that do not reach the reasoning mind. I believe that there was something of that here." She put down her pots, and offered William her arm. With relief, her gardener took over the work and, once the gentry had made some progress down the mall, re-arranged the planting by his own laws.

"I shall not keep house for Sir James Stokes. We shall go,

you and I, to the English Embassy, once, on some great occasion such as King George's birthday. We shall stay an hour and then you shall take me away."

"As you command, aunt. Sir James said that he could not, with honour, refuse the Embassy."

"I have heard that honour is important to English gentlemen," Mme Duclos said.

XI

The opportunity came not a week later. The occasion was a visit to Paris, in semi-incognito, by the Prince of Wales. William had the greatest misgivings about the English feast. He feared that, in the press and hullabaloo, his aunt would not be accorded the honour due her; or, worse, that Sir James Stokes might whisper *Nunc dimittis* and expire, taking down with him the rotten fabric of the European alliances. Conceited as he was, William thought his aunt had not reasoned all the possibilities.

He need not have troubled himself. Mme Duclos came down in a dress of grey silk, without jewels, and long gloves of the same mysterious colour. Ninnipen, the most policed of the Hurons, had exhumed and cleaned old Mme Neilson's coach, assembled a team and himself taken station on the box. At the hôtel Langlois, they waited in a line of vehicles for an hour. The evening was warm and windless. Mme Duclos showed no impatience.

At last they came under the carriage porch. Ninnipen sprang down, beat away the Embassy servants and opened the door. William and his aunt stepped through clouds of foot-men's powder into another crush, made up this time of pedestrians, the women brilliant as the flightless birds of the Tropics, the men all crosses, badges, plaques and parti-coloured sashes. In the ballroom, so tight was the press that had a needle dropped from heaven it would not have touched the floor. The heat was lethal.

"It is not good for me here, William. Let us return."

"Of course, aunt."

A foot-man blocked their way. He said in English: "Lieutenant Neilson, Hi his commanded to take you and Mrs Duclose to Is Hexcellency to be presented to Is Royal Eyeness."

Bugger, thought William.

As they battled through the throng, Mme Duclos said: "I hate this, William."

"I am sorry, aunt."

His heart burned for her, but also rejoiced. For the first time, Mme Duclos required his help. Their inequalities had vanished. They were pals on a jaunt through the whole country of Great Britain.

"I don't want to be presented."

"It shall be over in a moment."

At the head of the room, Sir James Stokes, in Court dress and stockings, was standing beside a young man beginning to spread at the waist, whom William took to be the Prince George Augustus Frederick of Wales. The gentleman wore the blue cordon of the Order of the Garter. Mme Duclos dropped a curtesie, William a bow. The Prince made an all but imperceptible motion of his head.

Sir James Stokes said in English: "May I present, sir, Mme Duclos and her nephew, my friend Lieutenant Neilson. They speak better English than I do."

"The stone-thrower?"

Address the lady, oaf.

Sir James intervened. "Mme Duclos's strength is the long sword, where she is peerless among all women."

A look of alarm passed over the Prince of Wales' face.

Mme Duclos smiled. "It is my nephew, sire, who commands our light artillery."

Sir James Stokes ascended to Great British heaven.

"Very nice, very nice," said the Prince. Of a sudden, he turned to the side. Mme Duclos made a second curtesie, and they stepped back. A path through the mob opened. William said:

"Now, who else of our friends is here?"

"Don't you dare, nephew."

In front of the *porte-cochère*, Ninnipen had not cared to advance the coach. He stood, face like a slab, arms crossed, amid a boiling froth of dismounted noblemen. Around and about, William heard: Who is the lady in the plain, but neat, slate-grey *tenue*? With the pleasant-looking young officer?

In the coach, Mme Duclos said: "What in Heaven caused Sir James Stokes to think I wished to be presented to the Prince of Wales?"

"It is his profession as a diplomatist, aunt, to display princes. Had he been a stockman he would have shown you his prize calf."

"I am not speaking to you any further, nephew. Oh, puppet . . ."

At the door of the porter's lodge, Mlle Isabelle was standing on one leg, in her night-gown.

"Did you see the Prince?"

"Yes. He is very handsome."

"And did you dance with him?"

"No, puppet. He was too kind to honour just one lady."

William had an epiphany. He saw why his aunt had refused the hospitality of her beloved friend, Mme Neiret, and brought the orphan girl to live with her. Mme Duclos needed a barricade against not her enemies but those, such as William and Sir James Stokes, Knight Commander of the Bath, who loved her.

"Did William dance?"

"Never!" he cried. "For he dances with but one lady. *Allons!*"

They began to spin in a dance from Québec that Mme Duclos had taught them.

"Oh, Ninnipen dear friend, will you not fetch my bag-pipes?"

The court began to stir. Men and women emerged, rubbing their eyes, some with instruments of music, others with wine and treats. The sound of boreal revelry, did it pass over the river and into the rue Saint-Honoré and trouble the sleep of princes?

The next morning, both aunt and nephew received cards from the British Minister to sup that day in private in the presence of His Royal Highness. Mme Duclos pleaded illness. William could not.

"I am sorry, William," she said.

"Do not be."

Redundant, William was seated down-table, amid secretaries, and learned something of the very violent exercise in practice among the scholars of Harrow School. A great distance away at the head came sounds of masculine laughter. They might have been at a cabaret at the Barrier. Only after the Prince had risen did Sir James Stokes seek William out. The tavern reek had blown off him and left no trace. His Excellency inquired after Mme Duclos's health.

"Old wounds, sir," William said with a malice he at once regretted.

"I know the sensation," said Sir James.

William very much liked Sir James Stokes, but no young man wishes to arrange the matrimonials of an older.

"Sir, I hope I shall have the honour of sometimes calling on you."

A look of pain crossed the English Minister's face and just as soon was gone.

"In large companies. That would please me."

XII

Mme Duclos was finding her new daughter a double-handful. Her scheme of education, precisely as she had received as a foundling from old Mme Neilson, broke down on its first experiment. Isabelle would barely write French, let alone Latin, and the sound of English and Italian caused her to wriggle. What she liked best was to dance and sing and shin up the plane-trees in the garden, free grapes from the glass-house, and play cassino in a roar. Read she would not, but loved to listen to her maman recite tales of knights and fair ladies. Mme Duclos became proficient in the novels of Mme de Tencin.

Isabelle loved the spectacle, whether Raucourt playing *Phèdre* at the Théatre-français, or a troupe of saltinbanques at the Fair. The child recognised no hierarchy of art any more than of society. Her heart was open to all. She was Gluckist and Piccinnist all in one.

Through the window, Mme Duclos watched her beloved, robed in a bed-sheet, eyes flashing, brows knit, left arm extended, in discourse with her attendants:

"Mes homicides mains, promptes à me venger,
Dans le sang innocent brûlent de se plonger."

My murderous hands are ready to avenge me.

They burn to plunge themselves in innocent blood.

A little later, the scene had been changed, and Isabelle was walking a tight-rope stretched between the plane-trees, her Huronne chorus ranged below to catch her should she over-balance.

Mme Duclos turned from the window and said: "Isabelle is not spoiled, William, for nothing could spoil such a pure spirit. Isabelle is indulged."

For the first time, William saw flecks of grey in his aunt's fine hair.

The lady was fortunate that, at every furlough, young William acted as relay. If, in her weekly letter, Mme Duclos wrote: "I believe my darling is beginning to settle down" or "Isabelle is becoming quite the *dame de cour*" then William knew that he was called to duty. They saw reviews at the Champ-de-Mars and boat-races on the Seine; attended the Italiens, the theatres of the Champs-élysées, the opera-ballet, the pantomimes at the Fairs, fireworks at the Étoile. They ate iced-creams at the Procope. Such entertainments, which might have compromised the reticence of Mme Duclos or disgusted his mother in their vulgarity, became delicious to William in the sparkle in the child's eyes.

The high day of the year was the Promenade of Longchamp. Years before, it had been the practice on the Wednesday of Holy Week to go out of town to hear the *Tenebrae* sung at the Royal Abbey of Sainte-Isabelle at Longchamp in the Bois de Boulogne, a distance of some four miles from the faubourg. In the way of such celebrations, the sacred purpose had been overwhelmed by a profane. The humble pilgrimage had become a procession of the finest equipages, the noblest teams, and the most beautiful women, stretching from the place Louis XV to the porte Maillot, down through the wood and back again. Mme Duclos detested all such show and but for the matronal saint would have embargoed her god-daughter from attending.

The day required from William the most meticulous staff work, for it was a day also for the humbler sort of Paris to see the fine ladies and cast aspersions or even stones at the turnouts. The theatres being closed for the festival, it was a chance to see Raucourt and other of the great *tragédiennes* who were not in the general habit of stepping into church and would not do so now.

From a class-mate now in the Maréchaussée, William arranged to have two saddle-horses brought to the porte

Maillot. Then, as the cavalcade and minutes passed, Isabelle and he would spring up and, abandoning the clogged carriage-ways, scamper over grass and under branches to the abbey, where Ninnipen was stationed to take charge of the horses and Sandoustie, the daintiest of his wives, dashed away with slippers, sponge and hair-brush. Then Isabelle broke loose, and flew up the nave, the tapers on the quire-stalls bending in two at her flight, while William clinked behind.

The outing always left the child pensive, torn as ever between the stage and the veil. Ahead in the gloaming trees, William could make out Sandoustie, riding pillion, her head against Ninnipen's broad back.

"Will you be my husband?"

"Isabelle! You shall decide on your husband when you are all-grown."

"Why?"

"You will surely meet a gentleman who is more handsome than I am and nearer to you in age. I am old."

"Maman wants me to marry you."

"Fibber! Your maman wants no such thing."

"I shall marry your friend."

"Which friend?"

"The blond."

"Count Bielke? He is in Russia. It is cold there, and there are wolves all over."

"I don't care."

XIII

The discoveries of the Messrs de Montgolfier, paper-makers of the Vivarais, had made a sensation through all Europe, but two years after the flight of their aerostatic machine, in the presence of His Majesty at Versailles, Paris was looking for some novelty in manned flight. Among people of science, the elasticity of the air trapped in the envelope and the weakness of the envelope itself had dimmed the ardour for *montgolfières*. The de Montgolfier brothers had shown that a machine might lift a body of considerable weight for a period. It could rise like a rocket and land in a heap. It could not be navigated. Lunardi in England and Zambeccari in Italy were hard on French anchor-ropes. The honour of French science was in play.

M. Fleurant, learned physician, modest and enlightened, proposed to the Academy of Sciences an innovation: that by means of sails attached to the gallery beneath the envelope of gas, the machine might be directed back to its place of ascension as a ship to its home port and brought safely to earth with the lightness, as he put it, of a sparrow on a roof-top. No more hard descents into fields and woods, to be anathematised by hedge-curates and pitch-forked by clowns!

The Champ-de-Mars, which had witnessed so many ascensions, was selected for the experimental flight. William's company was to guard the machine while it was filling with hot gas on the scaffold, while the other three cadet detachments would invigilate the spectators.

The day dawned fine and warm. The College Principal, equipped with a quadrant and a seconds-pendulum, took station on the dome of the College. Other gentlemen, similarly armed, were that moment ascending to the roof of the Observatory, the King's Wardrobe, the bell-tower of the Butchers' Church and the northern tower of the cathedral of Notre-Dame de Paris. The duc de Condé and four other noblemen were to be transported through the air and returned to their place of embarcation.

William noted from a distance that, even without their cordons and plaques, the gentlemen were broad about the middle. As they stepped up into the gallery beneath the envelope, the machine sagged, the gallery touched the boards and the ropes hung loose. There was a sort of grumble from the spectators. In a huff, the gentlemen stepped out and, with every appearance of dignity, never easy from beneath a globe of seventy feet in height and twenty-six in diameter, descended from the scaffold. The grumble became a roar of laughter.

Of a sudden, the attention of the crowd, as if it were a single mind like a bee-colony, turned to the middle of the field. A sun-burned lady was running across the open ground, wailing piteously. She seemed to William somewhat to resemble Sandoustie. She was Sandoustie. William raked the ground with his eyes and saw Isabelle, racing in a froth of skirts. She clambered onto the scaffold and sprang lightly over the balcony of the gallery.

"Take command, M. Davoust!"

William, too, was running, his sword beating against his ankles. The machine was gently lifting. At full stretch, he gripped the top of the gallery, and hauled himself up in a bundle. The machine halted for a moment, under the added weight, and then soared upwards.

William rose to his feet, put one hand on the gallery rail and shouted: "Mlle Duclos and Lieutenant Neilson at your service, sir!"

M. Fleurant bowed.

Isabelle was waving her bonnet and singing an ariette:

"Je m'élève au delà des airs
Et je plane sur l'univers"

I raise myself above the winds

And I glide across the Universe

"Attend to the fuel, if you please, mademoiselle."

"At your command, sir!"

At Isabelle's feet was a heap of little bricks formed, William suspected, from pressed horse-dung and straw. At full stretch, she fed the briquettes to the burner.

Looking down, William saw Paris as M. Turgot had imagined it in his famous plan. Churches, convents, streets, palaces and smoking chimneys were racing away from them. William thought: If we can navigate the air as easily as the sea, or more easily, what could humanity not achieve? A man might fly to Moscow and back in a day. And what a revolution in military affairs! A camp or fortress might be bombarded from the air as a sea-port from the water! Why do we do such things to make our lives more unhappy?

Isabelle had her hands to her ears. William was as cold as ice and gasping for breath.

M. Fleurant said: "We have reached the maximum elevation, where the elasticity of the atmosphere exactly matches that of the constrained gas."

And then: "M. Neilson! Your attention, if you please! Release your wing!"

William unwound a halyard from its cleat, matching M. Fleurant in every turn. William felt the wind snatch at the sail. The rope burned his palms and he released it.

"Bravo, M. Fleurant," Isabelle called out.

There was pandemonium. William saw, in billows of canvas, Isabelle sliding through a crater in the deck of the gallery. He threw himself down and pulled her by the hand to safety. Looking up, he saw the sail had come adrift and was hanging, helpless, from a single rope. Isabelle clambered to her feet.

The machine was spinning on its perpendicular axis. Witless from the wind, William drew sword and slashed at the ropes holding the second wing. The contraption slapped against the envelope and then fell, dragging its ropes, onto the city of Paris. The spinning slowed and then stopped. William caught his breath.

"M. Fleurant! The globe is pierced on this side!"

William saw, in the painted paper, a hole some ten feet by three feet.

M. Fleurant inspected the wound with interest.

He said: "Remark the invasion of cold air through the aperture. We are descending."

They were not descending. They were plummeting. William saw before him the towers of the castle of the Bastille.

William threw off his hat, sword and boots. Isabelle kicked out the remnant of the unburnt fuel, her slippers and a heap of flags. They scraped the battlements of the northeast tower of the castle, and then bumped over. The faubourg Saint-Antoine teemed and bustled below them. The houses were thinning. They cleared the place du Trône. Ahead, thank God, was the park of the royal hunting-place called the château de Vincennes.

William shouted: "When I say jump, jump, and not before!"

"I need to observe the landing," M. Fleurant said.

An immense shadow was bumping across the grass towards them. William took Isabelle's hand, which was small and firm.

"Knees bent! Relaxed as you can be!"

The shadow cleared a tussock and was on them.

They were in air, and the ground hit them. William lost his senses. With the return of sight and hearing, and feeling, or rather pain, in his hips and spine, William saw Isabelle was on her feet. Men and women were running across the grass like an army bent on pillage.

"Where is M. Fleurant?" Isabelle cried.

William rose with care. Fifty yards away, the envelope was burning. On his feet, hatless, without his wig, his coat in half and his breeches torn, M. Fleurant was regarding the wreckage.

M. Fleurant said: "A partial success."

Isabelle was engulfed by women and invisible for coats and ragged shawls.

A lady turned on William and stood with red hands on hips. She said: "Shame on you, sir, for risking the life of the little one!"

"Shame on the gentlemen!"

"Shame! Shame!"

Isabelle threw off her wrappers, tore away, spun on her toes and cried: "Hourra for M. Fleurant! Hourra for Lieutenant Neilson! Hourra! Hourra! Hourra!"

William had expected an evil quarter-hour at the rue Varenne, and he was not deceived.

Mme Duclos was standing at one of the windows of the saloon. Without turning, she said:

"Isabelle tells me you ascended from the Champ-de-Mars with M. Fleurant in an aerostatic machine."

"Yes, aunt. It was a partial success."

"Did you not think it your duty, sir, before exposing the child to such peril, to ask permission of her guardian?"

"I did think so, aunt, but also that you would refuse it."

Mme Duclos turned. Her face and eyes were without expression.

"In that, sir, you were correct."

"I did not think, aunt, that the risk to her was so . . ."

"Be quiet, sir, and listen to me."

Mme Duclos spoke.

"If you injure Isabelle, M. Neilson, do you know what I shall do to you?"

William felt the ice of Canada in his blood.

He said: "Yes, aunt."

"Let us speak no more of the incident, but thank God that you both are safe."

The Royal Porcelain Factory lies downstream from the city of Paris at the village of Sèvres. The director-general commanded from M. Falconet a dessert-plate entitled "The Ascent of M. Fleurant, Lieutenant Nelson and Mlle Duclos from the Champ-de-Mars in the aerostat *La Volante*, April 3rd, 1786. By privilege." Invited to the works to inspect the proof, William bought the whole firing, which charmed both artist and the direction-general of the factory. William returned at sundown with Ninnipen and a mason's cart. They loaded the crates of porcelain, drove a little way down the quay towards Saint-Cloud and smashed every dish into pieces lest some well-wisher send a specimen to Mme Duclos.

Such violence was uncalled for.

At the next visit, Mme Duclos said: "I must ask your pardon, nephew."

"There is nothing that Mme Duclos could ever say or do that would require my pardon."

Mme Duclos brushed away the compliment as if it had been a cobweb. She continued:

"The night of the ascent, Isabelle came into my bed-room and told me, in rivers of tears, that she had lied. Precisely: that you had done all in your power to stop her boarding the machine and only sprang up as it began to rise."

William said nothing.

"Isabelle said she feared I might be angry with her. I said that I was not and never would be angry with her but that I was angry with Cousin William.

"That injustice to her friend brought new torrents. We hugged and kissed, and, there and then, concerted that she would never again tell an untruth and her maman would never, ever be angry with Cousin William."

"I shall not give you cause, aunt."

Mme Duclos laughed. "M. Fleurant has pronounced the flight a partial success. I wonder what, for the gallant aeronaute, constitutes complete and utter failure."

William said: "Will you sit, aunt, for I have something to say to you."

"I can hear you as readily on my feet."

"M. Luynes killed a young girl at Québec. Mlle Adeline Bouchard, a pupil at the convent of the Ursuline sisters."

"I know, nephew."

A little vexed that his researches had yielded no novelty, William ploughed on: "I believe that is why General Neilson challenged him to fight in the place d'Armes."

"You are correct."

William gave up.

Mme Duclos said: "Before he went to America, M. Luynes attempted to abduct one of Mme Neilson's girl-servants. Mr Neilson vowed to fight him, but was forbidden by my maman. Instead, she ordered M. Luynes to America. When she read in Mr Neilson's memoire of the assassination of Mlle Bouchard, it broke her heart."

"Did the servant-girl at La Ferté live?"

Mme Duclos turned to face her nephew. "As you can see, by the grace of God, she does live."

XIV

Mme Neilson the younger was both an inveterate gossip and as discreet as the tomb. She might say, in a quiet moment, head-to-head, to some new favourite: Can you keep a secret? The young person would nod and lower her eyes. Then: "Better not, perhaps."

What opinions Mme Neilson held, or what tastes or pleasures she preferred, were always subordinate to the judgment of the Court and the fashionable world. Since she herself was one of the arbiters of good manners, or *bienséance* as she called it, she was required for ever to be alert to new precedents in the law of conduct or any additions to social law. She watched the conduct of her acquaintances at the Palace, at the ball or at the spectacle with that concentration a military officer brings to an intricate manoeuvre or a captain of vessel to a perilous in-shore passage; and always with the conviction that she was doing her duty to France, to history and to God.

"I cannot have that child blubbering in my loge."

As we have seen, Mme Neilson did not care for adopted children.

"Isabelle is musical, mother. The music touches her."

"Dearest, you do not attend the Opéra to listen to music. You attend the Opéra to support Her Majesty, to observe the best models of conduct and to learn how to present yourself in society."

Because of Suzanne, William found himself on shaky ground.

"You know best, mother."

Isabelle and William saw *Oedipe à Colonne* not from the

family's box in the first tier but standing in the *paradis*, below the ceiling, howling like babes.

William was ordered to Mézières. There, in that beautiful town at the very frontier of France, he entered a new world. Of all the technical schools, the Royal School of Engineering, founded in 1748, had the most brilliant reputation. A new world opened for William, not just in mathematical theory, but in practice. William learned to draw and create models of fortifications, and also to split wood and stone and to carry out chemical operations in a laboratory. All about were the great fortresses of Flanders, relics of the genius of the marquis de Vauban and the wars of the past century.

Each time that William saw Isabelle, she was altered. It was as if, in her progression from girl to woman, she was ascending in leaps. At each furlough, Isabelle was taller, more graceful, more womanly. Changes that might have escaped William's notice had he seen her every day now leaped at him.

Isabelle ran into the saloon to greet her cousin, but some invisible rein or halter now arrested her in mid-career. She no longer flew into his arms, but offered her hand. Her self-consciousness caused William to make an extravagant, almost Spanish obeisance, and click his heels together. Both laughed, laughter being the only exit from many such an embarrassment.

Their adolescence had raised a wall between them. Yet their recognition of it was a mark of their special understanding.

Often, when they were together, Isabelle fell into a sort of reverie which William did not like to disturb. He supposed that he, too, under the pressure of the military life, had altered: was neater in his dress, more precise in speech, gruffer, less playful, even more conceited.

William thought, as he rumbled back to barracks: What did you expect, idiot? That you and Isabelle would be falling hand-in-hand from aerostatic machines until Judgment Day? And you, Aunt Duclos, you have your *dame de cour*. What, precisely, shall you do with her? Then, diligent engineer that he was, William began sketching castles in Spain: the which, apprentice work, fell down at the first puff of powder.

XV

Absorbed in his work, his self-importance and, truth be told, his Iberian fortifications, William neglected his correspond-ence. He feared, also, that in writing to the rue Varenne, he might not keep command of his feelings. The spring had all but passed into summer before he noticed that, in turn, he had had no letter, either from Mme Duclos or from Isabelle.

He wrote to both and received no reply. He devised some business in the capital, and set off by post. At the rue Var-enne, he found his own way. In the saloon, he listened for Isabelle's running steps on the stairs. At length, his aunt entered. As he kissed her face, he felt at once an alteration, even a constraint, in her manner.

Summoning his military sang-froid, he said: "Is Isabelle away?"

Mme Duclos replied: "She is." And then: "Isabelle is married."

William's universe disintegrated. Scrabbling amid the rubble, he cried out: "Who has taken her from me?"

"Count Bielke."

"Why didn't you warn me, aunt?"

"I believed there would be a fight."

"There shall be, Mme Duclos. You may be quite sure of that."

It was not simply jealousy that another, and his friend, had what he could not have. William understood, for the first time, the meaning of the English sentence: *He had set his heart on her.* In all their jauntings and excursions, that was the secret. He also knew, with equivalent certainty, that his aunt had wished them wed.

"You shall not fight Count Bielke, nephew."

"And why not, aunt? He has stolen all my hope in life."

Mme Duclos said: "He has not stolen what was given him by a free and ardent will."

William believed that, but could not bear to think that Isabelle had preferred Pavel Sergueïevitch. He could not accept that and keep his masculinity intact.

Mme Duclos said: "Do you wish to injure her?"

"No, aunt. Never on my life."

"Then do not fight Count Bielke."

William blurted: "The lass will think I did not love her!"

"So be it."

"Aunt, I do not have your strength."

Mme Duclos took a step towards him. She touched him on the breast. "There! Such as it is, you have it."

To himself, William seemed to be drifting away from land, as if on a raft or piece of ice, with only his aunt watching from the *terra firma*.

Mme Duclos said: "You may not know, or may have forgotten, that I married M. Duclos against my god-mother's wishes. I . . ."

Mme Duclos put her hands to her face. She turned away and whispered: "She came so late and so early went."

Mme Duclos was as near to tears as William had ever seen her.

"I am sorry, aunt. Your loss is as great as mine, or greater."

Mme Duclos pulled herself together. "What I do know is that General Neilson, and my maman, were they here now, would say: In not challenging M. Bielke, you are doing the right thing for which, in the end, you shall be honoured."

"I shall not fight Count Bielke."

"And you shall live, nephew."

"I shall live, aunt, if that is what it is called."

Mme Duclos turned away. "The true reason is that Isabelle

must leave this unhappy country. For we are going into darkness."

She walked to her escritoire, unlocked one of the drawers, and brought out something wrapped in light paper. It was a handkerchief, much worn, frayed and repaired. On it, were the traces of the Joyeuse blazon, a white cup on a dark field.

"This is my most precious possession. General Neilson wore it sewn into his shirt above the heart. I wish you to have it as I believe he would have wished. It is our consolation."

XVI

All the same, the challenge was made, and not by William.

Whether for his birth, his father's reputation or the wisps of juvenile glory he had brought from the colleges, William was somewhat of a favourite of his brigade-colonel. On business in Paris, walking together in evening sunlight through the Palais Royal in pursuit of supper, William saw, at one of the *limonadiers* under the arcade, surrounded, as ever, by military parasites and flatterers, Count Bielke. William supposed that his enemy had stayed in Paris to receive his, William's, challenge.

William walked on. As he passed, Count Bielke, without rising from the table, picked up a glove in his fingers and tossed it towards William. The glove slapped against William's hip, hung a moment on his sword hilt, and then dropped to the ground.

Col. Beaulieu pointed with his cane at the glove on the ground.

William shook his head.

"I do not want you in my brigade."

"You have my resignation, sir, which I shall confirm in writing."

XVII

There is nothing so fatal to a military career as the taint of poltroonery. The institution of the duello, if it can be said to have any military purpose, is to keep that always before the eyes of officers.

A civil man, William left Paris and then France. For a time, he was in Holland, and then Germany. A letter from his father, in which as ever that officer neither praised nor blamed, found him at Brussels. There was a postscript, on a separate page, as if it had been an afterthought or so the leaf might be detached and destroyed. The postscript was in English. It said: "Fight once and for all."

Each day, William spent an hour at the shooting-range. One evening, in the buffet in the undercroft of the Town

House, William came on a group of noisy cavalry-men who, when they saw him, threw their gloves to the floor in peals of laughter.

Approaching the merry board, William said: "I accept the challenge. Shall I fight you all, or shall you elect a champion?"

Open mouths were closing. A big fellow with blond hair in curls retained the ghost of a smirk. William slapped him on the left cheek and drew blood.

At the meeting next morning, the witnesses attempted to compose the affair. William, who had no witness, refused and shot the poor man's head off. He had no more trouble of that sort except within himself, for he had become to himself a murderer. He thought to himself: How far must a man fall before he touches ground?

William did not think of Isabelle. He did not for a moment suspect that Count Bielke had married Isabelle for the same reason he had challenged him, William, to fight: to show the world that in their friendship there was not a trace of conventional sentiment. Count Bielke wooed and won Isabelle in the same spirit that he sold a fresh lieutenant a winded horse or bankrupted another, on the lad's first night in garrison, at the faro table. In reality, Count Bielke found, soon enough, that his bride was quite as wild as he was, and he laughed at the joke on himself. He had intended to run through Isabelle's money, and then see how they fared, but had not reckoned with Mme Duclos and the columns of sombre legal French-men at her elbow. He laughed at that, too.

The specific fault of royal life-guards since the Praetorians is conspiracy. The favour of the sovereign, their light or non-existent duties, their dazzling appointments, accommodations, mounts and uniforms breed in guards officers the conviction that they are best-equipped to select the ruler of the realm; and, in emergencies, or should the royal house lack candi-dates, take on the task themselves. That was as true in Tsarian Petersburg as in the saraï of the Ottoman Sultan and the palaces of the Caesars.

Captain Count Bielke drank. Bielke gamed. Bielke whored. Bielke did not plot. He could not be promoted, for some outrage would bring him sliding down to the ranks. Appointed *aide-de-camp* to Archduke Constantine, he was in post for six days. Yet old soldiers told recruits that, in a fight, they should look always to Count Bielke.

Maternity altered Isabelle as it does all but a very few women. The sleigh-rides at midnight that she had loved, the gun-play, wolf-hunts, pranks and theatricals vanished like tracks in a snow-fall. Bielke shrugged that off as lightly as her reforms on the farms at Olenskaïa Poliana. When Beetenschmecker, the German agricultural traveller, visited the estate during his Russian tour in the spring of 1788 and praised the enlightened management of the lands and the fair treatment of the labourers, the tables were turned at

Court and in the Mess. How his brother-officers praised that far-sighted, liberal and progressive proprietor, Count Bielke! Yet of all that gentleman's virtues, not the least was that he was never angered and never resented. Captain Count Bielke laughed.

Isabelle ceased to attend Court or visit Peter, lest some sympathetic lady tell her of her husband's love affairs. On her husband's visits, which were all the sweeter for being infrequent, Isabelle did not sulk or scold, for she knew his mistresses did that. Isabelle knew that she alone could bring up Count Bielke's children and manage his estate. Isabelle knew that she alone of womankind did not weary or annoy Count Bielke.

PART 2

The Englishman James Stokes

XVIII

In any society of men, constituted whether for business or for amusement, the ranks will derive their manners and pattern of work from their chief. If chief is idle, so are juniors; severe, likewise; frivolous, just the same; dissipated, as bad or worse. At the Embassy of His Britannic Majesty at Paris, habits of industry and probity, hitherto unknown in that place, had passed from Sir James Stokes to the grooms and scullions.

The secretaries and clerks early discovered that it was not enough to be punctual in their duties. They must, in super-addition, be unhappily in love with a French lady. Each sought, in his congenital manner, to fulfil both conditions of his office and, since the first was more readily achieved than the second, the business of the Embassy hummed. Not since the age of King Henry VI had the English in Paris spoken sweeter French.

At the same time, each youth attempted, according to his

own constitution, to capture Sir James' stooping walk and distracted air; his wealth, liberality and plebeian origins; his spotless moral character; and his solitary perambulations through the night streets of the capital. (They did not know it but their head was an assiduous attendant, under the name McCosh, at the meetings of the Scottish and Irish radicals at White's Hotel, place des Victoires, where he was notorious for advocating violent action.)

Rising late from their candle-trees, supping in fiacre, the lads haunted the Opéra and the theatres, raking the first-tier boxes with their glasses for a cruel countess to plunge them into misery. The correspondence with ministers in London, even in affairs of trade, was tinged with the melancholy of wasted vitality and frustrated promise.

As a body, those men and boys were schooled at unearthing intelligence. It was Mr Grundon who recollected, at the time of the visit of the Prince of Wales in 'Eighty-six, the lady in grey; and he had no sooner uttered his speculation that it became fact. Was it not the Stone-slinger who, that famous night, attended *La dame grise*? And so, link by link along the chains of reasoning and recollection, they came to William and then to Mme Duclos. Mr Tappin wondered aloud if their chief had met the lady in Canada; and then it came tumbling down like a box of toys and trinkets from atop a clothes-press.

Chapter-and-verse brought no relief, but rather a turn of

the screw. For if, amid the tapers and lights at the Comédie-française, one found a promising or potential Heartless One, would she also be expert in the Algonquian tongues; or skilled with the musket and blade; have fought three pitched battles; have navigated the length of the Saint-Jean river from its source; and still bear on her head an unpurged bounty of one thousand Spanish dollars? The statistical returns to London tailed away into reveries of self-extinction.

Then, one drizzle morning of that year 1788, the lady was there, in the *cour d'honneur*, in plain grey silk and veil, attended by a single sun-burned woman (Sandoustie); and here was Sir James Stokes, running down the stone steps to receive them. Being young themselves, the diplomatical spectators had, in their phantasies, made their idol young. They must needs adjust to a lady who had long entered her middle age, hair flecked with grey, well-shaped, erect in carriage and with that glamour of reticent persons, on their rare exposure to the public gaze, to draw the eye of every man, woman and child.

The interview was head-to-head. Chocolate was made but when it was brought up, the squaw-lady took charge with slaps. Raindrops spattered on the court. Without direct order, but as an instance of diplomatic prevention, the Ambassador's coach was washed and the team harnessed.

After an hour precise, the double doors swung in, the ladies came out, the one stepping out strongly, the other stamping and chattering. Footmen snapped. One bowed and lowered the coach steps but the ladies passed by and walked to the porter's gate, which closed behind them. The First Secretary turned from the window and lowered his hands in a piteous gesture of finality.

What occurred indoors was this. Mme Duclos sat down in an elbow-chair, and having been offered and accepted refreshment, said:

"May I speak, Sir James?"

"Whether you speak, Mme Duclos, or keep silence, I and this house are wholly at your service."

"I wish to petition His Britannic Majesty graciously to grant posthumous pardon to my late god-father, General Neilson."

Sir James Stokes was too complete a diplomatist, and too perfect a lover, to ask the lady why she should wish royal clemency for a man twenty-nine years under the frozen Canadian sod.

Mme Duclos proceeded. She said: "By reason of my criminal conduct in the battles for Canada, I believe I would hinder rather than advance such a petition. You, sir, have done my family such service in the past that I have no compunction in asking of you a further favour."

Sir James Stokes fought the inclination only to look at the speaker's face and let her voice play in his imagination. Yet habits of attention and analysis were not to be gainsaid. Sir

James Stokes thought: The storm is gathering and the lady needs the protection of Great Britain. Not for herself, indeed, for that is out of the question and, anyway, she is not not subject to fear for herself. She needs His Majesty's Ministers' protection for some connection of General Neilson. For her brother. Adoptive brother, to be precise. And his lady.

General Neilson's dying words came into Sir James' mind: Love my son.

It was the settled practice of Sir James Stokes to deal with a task or duty at the moment of its origination. Had he a discourse to make a year thence, he would write it straightaway and place it in the top-left drawer of his mirrored bureau. Was there some strand of cloud gathering over one of his secret agents, he would have her out to Spain and paid off, liberally.

Sir James began to speak in English. "In the action at Ticonderoga, which the French call Carillon, at great risk to his own safety, General Neilson frustrated the massacre of the British prisoners-of-war. He returned General Harris his sword without condition, and himself escorted that gallant officer to our lines at the south end of Lake George. Mr Neilson ensured that Gen. Harris' men were protected and himself acted as guarantor of their parole. Further, after our reverse at the Falls of Montmorency, in conjunction with Major Chumley, he supervised the exchange of prisoners on honourable terms."

If Mme Duclos was smiling at her host's stage-rehearsal, no trace of a smile surfaced to her lips.

Sir James Stokes continued: "The late Mr Harris told me, as he told others, that General Neilson was no adherent of the Pretender but had entered the French service for love of a respectable lady of that nation. By the fortunes of war, I was present at General Neilson's last moments on that glorious day before the walls of Québec, and never have I witnessed a man go to his Maker with greater firmness and Christian resignation.

"Sire, I make this plea wholly on my own impulse. If, in the course of my service, I have ever given cause for satisfaction . . ."

Sir James paused in his mental draft. Sandoustie was edging along the walls, peering into tobacco jars and snuff-boxes, opening the glass doors of clocks and spinning the hands, snapping at bell-ropes. She paused for some time before the red ribbon and badge of Sir James' order of chivalry, which hung in devil-may-care fashion from the frieze of a pier-glass. Sir James Stokes took a step towards the lady, rolled up the sash, and, with a compliment and his few words of Wendate, presented it. The trophy appeared to please the Huronne, for she concealed it in her dress.

Mme Duclos said: "Thank you, Sir James."

Mme Duclos stood up, turned to the door and then turned back. Mme Duclos said: "Shall we have fallen out, Sir James?"

Sir James Stokes nodded, sat down at his desk, and watched the ladies make their departure, unattended.

So it was that, while the chancellery grieved, Sir James Stokes had never in his life been so happy. As the reader will have deduced, His Britannic Majesty's Ambassador at Paris had not been born to high estate or even to the middling sort. He had made his plum by his own labour. To himself, James Stokes was still the Brentford guttersnipe who had scrabbled up to Westminster School and St John's College and would ever be so. He said to himself: "She'll have ye, Jacky, and then ye'd well look sharp."

It was at that moment, and for the first time, that Sir James Stokes felt his solitude which had been, as it were, his companion in life. The thought of being one day part of his late guest's whole existence spread out before his mind and heart a wasted lifetime. Work, which had ever been for him the sovereign remedy for all such thoughts, reclaimed him. He wrote, signed, sealed and despatched his letter to King George. All the while, he was asking himself: Why has Mme Duclos lost her faith in the royal government of France?

He returned to his desk. It was not that Mme Duclos had given him an idea. It was rather that a precipitate of political impressions, lying like a deposit on the floor of Sir James' intellect, had been stirred into motion.

Sir James Stokes addressed the Secretaries of State at length. Like some aerial witness, he ranged over the French finances: the failure of Bernard in 1709, the shipwreck of Mr Law's reforms in 1720, the lottery of 1757, the frustrations of Messrs Necker and Turgot, the Canadian bankruptcy and, now, the ruin of the King's Treasury in the American rebellion and war. At each crisis, the French Crown had saved itself but the longevity of an institution is not any guarantee of its permanence.

There was small or no chance that the Parlement of Paris would authorise the King to levy new taxes or permit the creation of additional venal offices or annuities. His Christian Majesty must needs, for the first time in one hundred and fifty years, to convene the Estates of France and that would bear consequences that neither he, Sir James, nor even the Lords Secretary could with confidence predict.

Sir James spread out before Their Lordships certain possible consequences. At the least, there would ensue some abridgement of the privileges of the nobility and clergy, and a corresponding expansion of the liberties of the Third Estate. There would be limits set on the royal prerogative. It was now of the first importance that His Britannic Majesty should have a clear idea of what the Third Estate would request or demand; and, for that reason, his servants in Paris would, without ostentation, frequent the clubs and societies of the men of that order. He, Sir James Stokes, would confine his activity to the Court.

The composition required all the day and evening. The

work might have proceeded more urgently had not every half-hour one of his people tip-toed in with some piddling inquiry. (The First Secretary had ordered the clerks to call on their chief in relays lest, in the shipwreck of his dreams, Sir James Stokes do himself lethal hurt.) Such interruptions did nothing to ruffle the Ambassador's famous courtesy.

"And Mr Grundon?"

"Yes, sir?"

"Will you do me a particular service?"

Mr Grundon feared a carpeting.

"Ye-es, sir."

"Will you go for me to Montauban?"

Not knowing how to answer, the youth said: "Sir, I have lately received a tender impression . . ."

"It is well that the lady should know that you put duty above all."

"Ye-es," poor Peter Grundon said. And then: "Shall you give me a chit on the cashier?"

"No, sir. I wish you to go on foot and without funds."

Mr Grundon said nothing.

"Go into the houses of the poor, sit on their beds, look into their cooking-pots, lie by their hearths, watch over their infants and parents. Taste their food and drink their water. Look closely at their eyes and their teeth. Examine their ploughs and their hoes. Come back when you have enough to say to me that would fill an half-hour."

"What about the returns, sir?"

"I shall do the statistical returns, Mr Grundon. Would you kindly ask Mr Tappin to come to me?"

"Mr Tappin is up next. In ten minutes by the clock."

"Very good."

It was the habit of the Embassy courier, otherwise steady in his work, when carrying letters to London he deemed to be of general or public interest, to make his way not to the ministers at White-Hall in the west of town but to Jonathan's Coffee-House in 'Change Alley in the City to the east, where he would share their import, for value, with the lounging stock-jobbers. (Sir James had tested a suspicion by inserting something fantastical in a despatch and read it, presented as scripture, three days later in the *Pall Mall Gazette*.)

Sir James Stokes consigned his day's work not to the cipher and the satchel but to memory, writing on a scrap of wastepaper the first two words of each paragraph should he need to jog that cerebral faculty. Mr Tappin tapped in and departed, five minutes later, for Rennes. Then Sir James Stokes burned in the fire-grate his brouillon and crossed the fire-irons over the flame lest some legible scrap pass up the chimney and out into the watching night. At eleven of the clock, His Britannic Majesty's plenipotentiary was seen to descend, plainly or even blackguardly dressed, carrying a portmanteau. Mr Grundon stalked his chief to the office of the Boulogne diligence, and watched him mount amid the lackeys and maidservants on the outside.

XIX

We return to the Champ-de-Mars of Paris, but not as we have seen it up to now. It is July 14th, 1790, the first anniversary of the attack on the Castle of the Bastille, and it is pouring with rain. It is the Feast of Federation.

Since before dawn, delegates from every corner of France have been streaming over a pontoon bridge from the right bank, singing *Ça ira* or stamping out the chain-dance called *la farandole*. The old exercise-ground has been transformed into an amphitheatre, with tiered banks on each side to accommodate the public and, at the south end, gay tribunes for the foreign envoys and the deputies of the Convention. Somewhere amid the three hundred thousand people, of all ages and sexes, unmindful of their tramp from every corner of the constitutional realm, or of the buckets of rain, intoxicated by the sense of being all of one mind and body, are the King and Queen, she with the little Dauphin in her arms.

In the middle of the amphitheatre, on a raised hillock, the Bishop of Autun is celebrating the Mass, surrounded by priests dressed in surplices turned transparent with moisture. Their stoles are embroidered with tricolores. Across the river to the north, the quai de Chaillot and the heights of Passy are teeming with colour and the wet smoke of picnic-fires.

On the edge of the crowd, a man and a woman, both in their middle years, stand apart from the crowd and give the impression of being more interested in each other than in the magnificent spectacle of national unity. Both wear the citizen's cocarde, he in his dripping bicorne hat, she on the stick of her parasol.

"One would have thought that the Supreme Being might have conceded better weather."

"It is possible the Reverend Bishop of Autun is celebrating the Mass backwards."

M. Talleyrand-Périgord, the bishop in question, is known rather for cunning than for sanctity.

To an impartial spectator, if there may be such with so much more novel and exhilarating round about, the pair have not the intimacy of lovers, nor the habitude of married persons or blood siblings. There is between them a depth of feeling arrested by reserve. Only an observer of experience would guess they are adoptive brother and sister.

The gentleman looks down and says: "There is nothing so absurd as new ceremonial. Who would have thought that we French, who fear ridicule above all things, should so embrace it?"

William Neilson the elder, camp-marshal of artillery, believed that the revolution in French politics did not greatly concern him. The debates in the Legislative Assembly, the different sects and wings at one another's throats, the marches and proliferating news-sheets were to him like the midnight tiffs of fellow-travellers in the next room at the Post-inn. His affair was the artillery branch of the army.

Like many active officers, William had been frustrated by the venality and nepotism of the old military establishment. During the session of the Estates-General, he had hoped that a constitutional monarchy, in the manner of England, might bring efficiencies and introduce good men into the finances and military affairs, but without the accursed party feeling of Great Britain.

A wider franchise and a scheme of taxation acceptable to the public would, M. Neilson believed, re-inforce the progress of the last years: the re-construction of the navy and the merchant marine, new carriage roads radiating out from Paris, canals like veins of silver through the French earth, advances in natural science, chemistry and aeronautics. By temperament and formation, William thought in categories of organisation, not in the new language of rights brought over from America. In truth, he thought that there were no rights even for the King: simply a succession of truces between the different interests in society. People spoke of liberty, but what they wanted was property and power, for that is what everybody wants.

He thought the attack on the castle of the Bastille

infantile, and its demolition beyond incompetent. The new words flying at him – aristocrat, anarchist, vandal, revolution, counter-revolution –, the dubious paper-money and the cloacal language of *Le Père Duchesne* bored him. (There is nothing so contemptible as the affectation, in a journalist, of what he thinks is the speech of the back-alleys.) Where others saw patriots, M. Neilson saw notaries without business, priests without parishes, poets without printers, playwrights without plays, teachers without pupils, journalists without journals, physicians without patients. The Marshal had thought an Enemy of the People was a Prussian or an Englishman, not any person who disagreed with Messrs Robespierre and Saint-Just.

France was living out a history that was everybody's but its own. Every man and woman was on stilts. If he was a Brutus in a toga, she was a Cornelia, with a high waist and bare arms and bosom. William's concern was the efficiency of his foundries and formations. And, naturally, the safety of his family.

"Mme Neilson is an entire stranger to fear, Sister Duclos. It is one of her many admirable traits of character."

"That is why you must go across the water. All of you, except young William."

William Neilson shook his head. "What have we to fear? Mother freed the blacks in the île de France and defied the King in the matter of the Canadian debts. She introduced

Mr Hume and Dr Smith to Paris, saved poor d'Alembert from famine, wrote the article on Heat in the *Encyclopédie*. If anybody belonged to the *parti philosophique*, it was mother."

There was a flash of sunlight. Marshal Neilson said: "Anyway, the storm has passed."

The heavens chose to differ in a burst of thunder and rain.

"Evidently not, brother."

"I shall not bear arms against France whatsoever her government."

"That shall not be required. You shall live quietly. I have money in the English funds."

Brother William raised a hand, for so had he, and a great deal more.

He smiled and said: "I cannot imagine Mme Neilson thriving in North Berwick."

"You must tell Mme Neilson that if she does not go to England or Scotland, she shall lose her life and those of her children."

"Our property will be taken. Like the poor priests."

"Not if you pass it to young William, as I have done."

Marshal Neilson nodded. He had had that thought.

"And you, sister?"

"I have told Sir James Stokes that I will be his wife, and love and care for him."

William Neilson the elder chose his words with care.

At length, he said: "My sister, Sir James Stokes cannot with honour demand your hand as the price of Mme Neilson's safety."

Marshal Neilson had never seen his sister so flare up.

"You speak only of Sir James' honour, William Neilson. Do not women have honour? Captain Stokes gave us escort to carry father's bier into the city of Québec. At the île Sainte-Hélène, he conveyed my request for an half-hour's grace to Mr Amherst, although he knew very well that I intended to take our people out. He was forced by General Amherst's animosity to sell his captain's commission and leave the English army. He now proposes to issue papers of naturalisation for you all. Do you not think, M. William, that the least I can do in return is to brush Sir James' coat each morning?"

William had an idea that something more was required of a dutiful wife.

"So you will go to London also, sister?"

Mme Duclos shook her head. "I am a fugitive from English justice. Because of my crimes in Canada, there is a bounty on my head. I am safe, for the moment, only in France."

They were silent for a while.

"It will break my heart not to see my sister again, or young William."

"We shall meet again. Nothing that is excessive can be permanent. In time, everything returns to equilibrium."

XX

William's mother became more and more outspoken. At a performance of *Iphigénie en Aulide*, at the chorus of "Let us sing! Let us celebrate our Queen!", Mme Neilson stood up and applauded. The parterrians did not care for that, and Marshal Neilson had to shield his lady from a hail of fruit-skins and pen-knives. The performance was halted. The *Chronique de Paris* did not name the loyalist lady, but all Paris knew it was Mme Neilson.

As everybody knows, at mid-summer of 1791, the King and Queen left Paris in disguise and attempted to reach the town of Montmédy on the eastern frontier and the protection of General de Bouillé and a garrison of loyal regulars. Some fifty miles short of that place, the post-master at Sainte Menehould recognised the King from his portrait on the paper-money, and the family were sent back under armed escort to the sullen capital. Sir James Stokes, who had no prevision of the escapade and would have pleaded against it, saw that the constitutional monarchy was doomed. The King of Prussia and the Holy Roman Emperor threatened consequences if the royal family were further mistreated. Certain that war was inevitable, young William, who was doing very little in Warsaw, returned to his homeland to enlist.

On August 10, 1792, popular militias attacked the Tuileries and slaughtered the Swiss guards. The royal family took refuge in the session of the National Assembly in the riding-school the other side of the palace garden. They were transferred from there to the Temple prison. For their better security, a ditch was dug around the gloomy old tower.

On the 17th, Sir James Stokes received orders from Secretary Dundas to request his passports. Since it appeared, Mr Dundas wrote, that executive power had been withdrawn from His Very Christian Majesty, Sir James' credential was now void. His Britannic Majesty had therefore thought it proper that His Excellency no longer remain in Paris. At the same time, His Excellency should take every opportunity of expressing that, while His Majesty intends strictly to adhere to the principles of neutrality he has observed in the matter of the internal government of France, he believes it no deviation from those principles to express his solicitude for the personal situation of Their Christian Majesties and the royal family.

Sir James wrote back in cipher that such a step would be interpreted as tantamount to a British declaration of war, and would prejudice the safety of the King and Queen of France. He begged to be permitted to remain in the country in a subordinate character. He was refused.

On August 28th, the English Embassy drove out of Paris in a hail of horse-dung and stones. The convoy was held for a day and at night at Valenciennes, on the frontier of the Austrian Netherlands, while the passengers' passports were inspected and their baggage unpacked and scattered in the dust. Among the voyagers was Mr MacNeill, Scottish, his wife (whose lower face was bandaged by reason of a tooth abscess), three small children and a servant, John. On September 20th, at Valmy in wooded country in Champagne, young William had his first taste of battle when the volunteer battalions (supported, it must be said, by regulars and his father's artillery) chased off a Prussian army under the Duke of Brunswick. He discharged his arm just once. Astonished and elated by the victory, the Assembly two days later declared that France was henceforth a Republic.

It was the Neilson family's good fortune that the Sologne was an area remote from democracy. Even Orléans had not the ferment, either popular or royalist, of Lyons or the western departments. Far from being hated by the country folk, the Neilson family was honoured. Old Mme Neilson had, in the later years of the Old Régime, dug a canal of communication and irrigation for the use of the district, and her successors maintained the works without charge. The tenants, many of them Germans from the Palatinate, owed their farms and Frenchness to that lady. The family had also learned, over its ten centuries of existence, how to turn in the prevailing winds, like the tricolores snapping over the four towers of La Ferté-Joyeuse.

As much to the point, the woods about the mad old castle were known to be the haunt of wild men who paid no taxes and owed no loyalty to crown or republic. In the turmoil of that August of 1792, M. Ballin, son of old Mme Neilson's steward or *intendant*, came from Orléans into the woods to make a survey of the timber to be cut for his profit. He was found, many weeks later, hanging from a branch of a great oak, strangled and scalped. Few men dared to enter the woods in sunshine, and none after nightfall.

It was young William's good fortune that the Assembly resolved to support the armies on the Rhine with a corps of engineers dedicated to river crossings. They became known as pontonniers. It was not a specialism apt to attract gentlemen or even ambitious new men. When asked why he should wish to lash boats together, William responded, with a conceit even he found insufferable, that one must fight the present and not the last war. The saying, for all its vacuity, gained currency and William had it said back at him, and more than once.

By an inadvertence, or out of national feeling, William was entered in the list at Strasbourg not as the barbarous Neilson but as Niellon, a name not uncommon in the duchy of Burgundy and elsewhere. Having no wish to bear a family name he believed he had shamed, William accepted to be Niellon. The past was being destroyed before his eyes, prisoners massacred, castles and convents demolished, his mother and father in exile, all officers of noble birth reduced to the ranks. The eradication of private sentiments in an identity of national purpose suited William. If William had much to hide, so did many others.

In Strasbourg, he found the corps of pontonniers, modest and stoical and Dutch, much to his taste. The country charmed him, with its terraced vines and crazy inns where he drank wine that seemed but an amalgam of rain and sunshine and caused no intoxication.

Knowing both English and High German, William found it no great labour to master the intervening language; and all the more since the Dutch men conversed in a few profanities that were readily committed to memory. There were no hierarchies or fixed ways of doing things, no strutting officers with white epaulettes and the fleur-de-lys on their buttons, but also no sneaking *sans-culottes*. The Representatives of the People Among the Armies (as they were termed) stalked other companies, but those exquisites did not trouble themselves with a motley collection of Dutchmen.

By the franchise of the men, William was elected sergeant and, a little later, once again commissioned lieutenant.

PART 3

The Letter Office

XXI

As will be recalled, Sir James Stokes was given his passports and left France in August of 1792. He disappeared from view. It was said that His Britannic Majesty was displeased at not having received from his Ambassador at Paris earlier intelligence of the revolution in French politics. (In truth, His Majesty had been ill and had not heard, through the tumult in his brain, the reading of his envoy's despatches from Paris.) Sir James Stokes was forbidden to present himself at the Levy or the Drawing-Room at St James' Palace. Spared the gloom, filth and crush of that royal hovel, the former envoy was said to be enjoying his disgrace in Montgomeryshire.

Towards the end of that year 1792, a young member of parliament, Mr Covington, who had a notion to make a name for himself in postal affairs, was beating through the list of General Post Office sinecures, when he came on the title: foreign secretary, *£25,346 7s 11d*. In the House, he rose in the smoke and lamp-light and asked a question. Flustered, the Chancellor of the Exchequer referred the matter to the Secretaries of State. That same night, returning to his rooms in the apartments in Piccadilly known as Albany, elated by the slaps and punches of his allies, and, if truth be told, more than a little light of head, young Covington found a gentleman standing beside the cold fire-grate.

Sir James Stokes said: "I am Godfrey, foreign secretary of the General Post Office, Mr Covington. I understand you had a question for me."

"How the deuce did you get in, sir?"

"I opened the door, Mr Covington."

Which was true.

Mr Godfrey's department, at those sparse moments when it answered to name, was known as "the private foreign office", "the foreign secretary's office", "the foreign department" and "the foreign letter office". Established at the General Post Office on the eve of the Jacobite rebellion of 1715, its business was to open mail to foreign embassies or persons of interest, decipher the merchant cant or cyphers devised by the Stuarts and the other continental Courts, copy the screed, reseal the original and forward it to its legitimate destination.

With the convulsions of 1792, the arrest of the French King and Queen, and the declaration of the French Republic, Parliament enacted two measures, the Westminster

Police Act and the Aliens Act, to scotch or quarantine any levelling contagion from across the English Channel. England, which was for ever vaunting its liberties, now had a secret police as comprehensive and sinister as those of France and Russia. The letter office was suppressed and its seals transferred to the new Aliens Office.

Except they were not.

At his withdrawal from Paris on that August 28th of 1792, Sir James Stokes took leave of his people at The Nore, alighted on the Medway, and came into London by way of Rochester and Chatham. He went straightaway to Secretary Dundas.

For himself, Sir James Stokes had no especial desire to preserve the fantastical edifice of prerogative, corruption, patronage and nepotism that had raised Great Britain to the foremost rank of nations. He did wish to preserve Mme Duclos and his friend, the Stone-thrower. He asked the Secretary of State that he might be permitted to return to France, under legend, as a delegate to the Convention from some remote and rural *département* such as the Cevennes. He would thus have opportunity to observe the principal actors in the drama unfolding in Paris.

"Hoots, Jackie, ye're a braw ane," Secretary Dundas said. "And a fule."

Instead, Sir James Stokes was given a name, an apartment of three rooms at the General Post Office in the City of London, as many clerks and couriers as he required, the packet-boats from Dover, Harwich and Falmouth, and a secret title for funds.

The General Post Office of Great Britain occupied a crazy, old merchant's house in Lombard Street, abutting at its west end the beautiful square church of St Mary Woolnoth. It was a twisting, dark road of tall houses of blackened brick, the lower storey spattered with mud and, even in day-time, tallow-candles flickering through sea-green panes. This dismal thoroughfare came to life twice a day, at dawn and at midnight, in a blare of horns and the crash of lathered horses stumbling through the fog.

The abolition of the foreign letter office had transformed the heritable G.P.O. sinecures into pensions. The clerks, most of them French Protestants in exile, all Freemasons, that had held their places by patent for three-quarters of a century, were released into pasture. Their successors now worked "at pleasure", as we say; the pleasure in question being not that of the King but of foreign secretary Godfrey.

Mr Godfrey dug out Tim Tappin and Peter Grundon. They had advanced no further into the capital of Great Britain than the inns of Rotherhithe and Limehouse, respectively. Mr Godfrey found them in the final stages of gin-dementia. Dried out, and relieved of their French amatory labours, the lads gave full attention to their work.

The custom of the office was to use the best Amsterdam sealing-wax, at five guilders per pound. Mr Godfrey ordered that the wax of each letter be taken off, labelled and isolated; and then melted again for the re-sealing. He diverged from that economy in the matter of the seal matrices. As copier and engraver of seals, the foreign secretary had enticed from Antwerp an elderly gem-cutter he had known in his business life, Mr Silva. Poor Mr Silva was obliged to account at the end of the day for every piece of cornelian he had cut and then to watch the stones, one by one, smashed to crumbs before his eyes. The clerks wore linen footmen's gloves, a fresh pair each morning and each evening. (They were washed without soap by Mr Grundon's mother in Hoxton.)

The decipherers were, by that same custom of the office, reverend gentlemen, who chose to work on the interceptions in their parsonages or their rooms at Oxford. They were not as rapid as Mr Godfrey preferred. Every hour they detached from the ciphers and bestowed on their sermons, the Minor Latin Poets or their rose-beds impaired the value of the intelligence. He sent Tim Tappin to Hanover, to learn deciphering under the learned Herr Bode. As much to the point, young Tappin was to open a sluice or side-channel to draw off the German interceptions, which His Majesty of Great Britain and Elector of Hanover had been wont, selfish prince, to keep to himself. Some of the more economical European Courts re-used their ciphers, which hurried things along.

The clerks pursued their existence in an apartment on the ground floor of the Lombard Street house, on the west side of the court-yard. They entered not from the street, but from a wretched alley to the east called Abchurch Lane. The apartment consisted of one small room, always with a fire and candles burning, made smaller by a large circular table and a letter rack, known as the Alphabet, under the charge of Mr Grundon. Mr Silva had to himself a second room with a high window. The third room, smaller still, was reserved for the clerk-in-waiting, who stayed up the night to receive and open Expresses and, during the day, made himself obnoxious by lavish displays of indolence. The lads might take the air, not through the door on Lombard Street, but by the coach-arch into Abchurch Lane.

On the four Post days, the lads, blasted from their beds by the sound of wheels and horns, would scrabble down to find the foreign secretary already seated at the great table. From the heap of foreign letters, rarely fewer than a thousand, they made a selection. Of the chief courts, the French was of prime interest, but also the Prussian, Russian and Austrian, and sometimes the Swedish, Dutch and Sardinian. The diplomatic letters were all opened, copied, re-sealed and on their way by ten of the clock of St Mary, for Mr Godfrey thought it a mere courtesy that the foreign missions should be first in the capital to receive their correspondence.

On Friday night, after the coaches had rolled away, Mr Godfrey ordered wine and supper from Pontacks in the lane, which boasted of a French style of cookery though it was not at all French. Only Mr Silva, devoted in the matter of his nation's Sabbath, failed the orgy. The talk was "shop". The lads spun yarns, but not of their ingenuity or daring, but of incompetence beyond belief and shameful poltroonery. Mr Godfrey listened and smiled. On the two days without post, and on Sundays, the lads rested, as Our Maker rested after the Creation. As for Mr Godfrey, he never walked out in day-light. The clerks supposed that, as at Paris, he prowled the night streets, thinking of his love.

"I fail to see, Mr Godfrey," said Mr Covington, every atom the Parliamentarian, "how the rental of three rooms and the wages of eight clerks on the establishment can consume £25,000 in a calendar year. From the revenue of the Post Office and, after 1761, the Exchequer, the foreign secretary never required more than £9,000."

"I take no salary, Mr Covington, and use no franks. My people must be paid, Mr Covington. They are men of business, not of fashion. Their duty is laborious and not at all genteel. As for the packet-boats, good sailors are paid thirty shillings a month."

Mr Covington began to swell with his reply, but Mr Godfrey forestalled him: "To that must be added the expense of the foreign correspondents."

"I would have thought, sir," replied the democrat, "that those gentlemen would serve the United Kingdom as loyal subjects of the King."

"None is subject to His Majesty, Mr Covington, and none is a gentleman, though many are ladies. The Rotterdam Agency, which casts up the intelligence on maritime movements from the French ports, has a roster of six. Those persons must be paid. You will find, if we continue our intercourse, that pay, and good pay at that, is the only sound foundation of secret work."

"You are a Cynicist, Mr Godfrey."

"With respect, Mr Covington, I am not. There are very few persons of our times who have no use for money, whether in fact or in their imaginations. Money is the only certain value in this world below."

Mr Godfrey, who had been both poor to the point of famine and rich beyond any sublunary need, was well advanced in chrematistics. None the less, he saw that he had strayed off-course.

The foreign secretary took a new tack. He said: "My chief concern, or rather my only concern, is the security of the Post Office. If the continental Courts or the American States suspect for a moment the activities of our department, they will send their confidential despatches by messenger. Not five people outside the office know of this work. Six, now."

Mr Godfrey looked with kindness at his host. "I am afraid, sir, that you may not speak of this business even to your wife. I have given you a secret that you must bear to the grave, Mr Covington."

And then: "Do you understand, Mr Covington?"

Mr Covington was silent. He did not know that those five persons, or six by then, did not include His Majesty the King of Great Britain and Ireland and Elector of Hanover.

"You must prepare yourself, Mr Covington. When war is declared . . ."

"There shall be no war, sir."

Mr Godfrey corrected himself. "In the event that France declares war, and Messrs Chauvelin and Talleyrand request their pass-ports, I shall need houses in the Low Countries, probably Maastricht, at Lisbon and at New-York."

Mr Covington, who had thought the foreign office was but a branch of the revenue, could see very well that the establishment had nothing to do with the prompt and secure transmission of written letters. He was dazzled by haggard gleams of a secret world: laborious, unchaste, delinquent, polyglottic, and perilous beyond description. Mr Godfrey had not the brusquery of a military man nor that facility, a simultaneous deference and self-assurance, that British public servants had brought to perfection. Truth be told, Mr Covington was frightened of Mr Godfrey.

At their next meeting, on the foreign secretary's suggestion, and so there should be no colour of party preference, Mr Covington brought his pair, Mr Shelby. Each was met, in the hullaballoo of Old Palace Yard, by a veteran guardsman who lit them to wherever Mr Godfrey chanced that night to be residing. That first night in Upper Street, Islington, outside the slimy cottage, the parliamentarians shook hands.

"It was for this, dear enemy," Mr Shelby said, "that I came into the House."

That was not in the least true. Mr Shelby had pestered Lord Louth for one of his Seats because only Parliamentary immunity would preserve him from the King's Bench prison for debtors. For all that, the sentiment was sincere. Mr Godfrey controlled the corporation Borough of Harwich, where fully seventeen of the thirty-two electors were packet-men, and that was of interest to his parliamentary guests. The Earl of Louth was a miser and a bully. Each night, as he returned from His Lordship's board as hungry and thirsty as at his arrival five hours earlier, and stepped over the dun on his door-step, Anthony Shelby thought: Here is no sort of life.

There is, perhaps, no more certain means to bind a man in loyalty than to give him something to do. The foreign secretary asked Mr Covington to travel to Helvetsluys to pass a package to the skipper of the yacht *Elsa*. The box concealed but a paving-stone from the stable-yard in Lombard Street but was delivered with both seals unbroken. Mr Shelby, who was unmarried, boarded H.M.S. *Latona*, in funds, to escort a lady from Corunna to Portsmouth. Doña B— reported that, even at those moments when a gentleman is most apt to open his heart to a lady, her escort had let fall no hint of the *calle Lombardo.*

From his education as a "shy-cock", as we say, where for six years he had not stepped from his house in Kensington in day-light, had kept two trained mastiffs in the yard and had not permitted his girl to admit even the baker's lad lest he be the bailiff incognito, Mr Shelby had been bred, as if by premonition, for the secret life. His debts were consolidated, the arrears purged and the interest paid each Quarter Day. The principal remained, like a martingale or throat-rein on a high-spirited horse.

The rehearsals satisfactory, Sir James added the two members to the company. On January 21st, 1793, King Louis XVI of the French or Citizen Capet, as he was now styled, was killed by guillotine. Mr Godfrey believed the war would not be soon over. He had a new sensation, of weariness in the afternoon, which he feared was the weight of his sixty years. He was thinking of his succession. Neither of the Parliament men could manage the foreign office alone; but together?

In the House, the questions came fast and hard. Mr Covington bowled at the head. Mr Shelby struck the ball over the boundary. Their exchanges peopled the green benches rather more than might have been presumed for postal affairs. Both sides of the House believed that, some misty morning on Barnes Common or Hounslow Heath, there must be shots discharged and received. None remarked that the battles were all of Inland: on the dishonesty of the Deputies on the main roads, the broken horses and bad coaches, the slowness of the Cross- and Bye-posts. Of the foreign letter office, there was no word.

The House of Commons of Great Britain is better famed for eloquence than for conveniency. Accommodated in the old chapel of Saint Stephen in the Palace of Westminster, the hall is dark by day and smokey by night. The genius of Sir Christopher Wren had brought touches of elegance to the ceiling and the iron pillars supporting it, but the place still reeked of broadswords and Magna Carta. There was but one way in and one way out.

During the division on the Sedition Bill, in the crush at the door, Mr Shelby found himself beside the Prime Minister.

"Thank you, Mr Shelby," Mr Pitt said, without looking up. And then, since they were overheard: "For the moment, I can do nothing for you, sir."

Our friend, expanding to the limit of his new character, replied: "That is more than enough, sir."

That evening, at Louth House on the north side of Piccadilly, from the depths of the table, Mr Shelby felt Harwich overrun his soul. In his mind's eye, he was carrying barley down the Navigation of the Stour. With his own hands, he closed and opened the locks at Stratford and Dedham. He heard the plash of wheel at Flatford Mill, was dazzled by the sun off the mud at Manningtree, heard the distant reports of wild-fowlers stranded in their punts. In the estuary, the wind got up, and he glided past the Orwell, bringing its tribute of the effluvia of Ipswich, and, beyond the Harbour Fort, espied the North Sea.

"Mr Putney, will you not circulate His Lordship's wine?"

Mr Putney, under-secretary in the Home Department and a man of strong but not lively parts, looked to his left. The Earl of Louth was horizontal in his elbow-chair, mute and immobile. The decanter was launched down the table. It snagged on every hand but reached our friend without taking hurt to vessel or cargo. Mr Shelby poured himself a bumper, stood and raised his glass to his host.

"To Victory!"

The other gentlemen, excepting only His Lordship, pushed back their chairs and rose.

"To Victory!" they croaked.

XXII

In July 1794, or thermidor an 11 by the winsome new Republican calendar, William Niellon was ordered to Paris to take delivery of two thousand pounds of black powder. The Poudrerie had been established in the old château de Grenelle, in the fields beyond his old college on the left bank of the river.

A line of some twenty carts waited in the heat to be loaded. Women moved down the line, hawking eau-de-vie, tobacco, sausage, cheese and white bread. Servant-girls dallied and flirted on their errands. All was confusion in an inferno of smoke and dust.

"Put that out!"

A *cantinière* was sucking on the short tobacco pipe that we call a *brûle-gueule*, or "gob-burner". William knocked the pipe from the lady's mouth and ground out the fire with his heel.

"You prick!"

"Fucking pig-fucker! Fucking royalist pig-buggerer!"

"Unwiped Federalist ass-hole!"

"Ladies! What is this commotion?"

William turned from the insulted ladies and faced a civilian gentleman, his hat and coat speckled with dust.

"Are you the general director here, sir?"

"I am Chaptal."

"I had, sir, some recommendations for the better security of this place, but it would be impertinent to voice them to the greatest chemist of the age. I am good only for knocking pipes out of mouths."

M. Chaptal turned away and put some distance between himself and the molten ladies. William followed him.

The chemist had his head down. Without raising it, he said: "When, in Year 1 of our rational new calendar, Citizen

Carnot ordered me to establish the factory, I engaged to deliver each day a maximum of eight thousand pounds of combustive powder. Every emplacement at the factory was determined by that maximum. The work-shops were dispersed at a regulated distance apart, so that if fire caught in one building it would not spread to the others. Materials passed through the factory in a precise and invariable chain. I hired as labourers steady old soldiers who neither smoked nor drank wine, and thought that making black powder in Paris was more to be preferred than receiving it from the Prussians on the Rhine.

"In Year II, the Committee of Public Safety, under the pressing need of the army, ordered me to raise the fabrication to sixteen thousands. I pleaded that the site was quite unsuited for such an augmented volume. In erecting additional buildings between the existing work-shops, I would disrupt the processes of production and introduce an intolerable risk of accident. I was unsuccessful. Orders are orders.

"Then, with the campaign in Flanders, I was ordered to double the fabrication once again, to thirty-two thousands. Look about you, young man."

M. Chaptal raised his head and swept the scene with his arm.

"No order, no oversight, no system. Injuries every day. Twelve hundred cartmen, masons, plasterers, carpenters, metal-workers, drink-sellers and servants on errands mingling promiscuously with two-and-a-half thousand powder-makers. Wagons charged to the head with stones and lime crashing through court-yards where my men are rolling barrels of powder. In every doorway, a builder blazing away at his pipe. No security of accounts. Unremitting pilferage of charcoal, fire-wood, sulphur and powder. I regard it as a miracle, young sir, that we have been eight months without catastrophe. I treat each morning as my last."

M. Chaptal had tears in his eyes. He turned and walked into the pandemonium.

William knew, better than any Frenchman but M. Fleurant, that the prevailing wind in Paris is from the west. A fire from the factory would be in the rue Varenne in minutes. Leaving the sergeants to hear the ladies' closing arguments, William set off for that street, at the double, to warn his aunt of the Vesuvio half-a-mile upwind.

He found his old haunt a dismal place, the road scattered with rubbish, the walls streaked with excrement, the hôtels chained and sealed, their courtyard walls scratched with obscenities.

On the stairs of his house, William again smelled burning. In fright, he clattered up to the first floor, sword drawn, and with his boot kicked open the saloon door. The curtains were closed. In the faint light, William made out his aunt seated on a chair. She was dressed in an old-fashioned soldier's dress, none too clean, with red cartridge-pockets and arm-cuffs. About her, the native men were seated on the floor. M. Ninnipen was speaking in a foreign language.

William kneeled among the Canadians on the boards. The calumet passed to him, and he took two deep draughts. The room revolved on its perpendicular axis, and then on its horizontal. It righted itself. Ninnipen raised his arms and said:

"*Courage petit reste de la Nation huronne! Vostre tige n'est pas encore seiche, elle repoussera, Jesus resuscité la fera revivre et refleurir; ouy, Jesus la rétablira et rendra plus nombreuse que jamais!*"

Courage, little remnant of the Huron Nation! Your stock still has traces of moisture. It will push through to the surface. The risen Christ will make it live again and flourish again. Yes, Jesus will revive us and make us more populous than we ever were!

There were shouts of assent. Aunt Duclos rose from her chair, and all stood.

When the men had left, Mme Duclos said:

"William, you shall have no part in this."

"On the contrary."

"We shall not survive."

"Well, then, let me be permitted to die with my friends. It is a small loss to the Republic."

Mme Duclos said: "Mme de Thelles and the sisters of the convent are in prison at Compiègne. Having refused the generous offer of liberation from their sad confinement, and a small pension, according to the decrees of October 14th, 1790 and August 17th, 1792, the women have persisted in their puerile and fanatical fancies, and secretly conduct intrigues in the support of the former royal family. They are held in the Conciergerie, where this morning they cut their hair with their own hands so that they would not be touched by the prison barber. They are to go before the Tribunal on Monday at dawn and from there to execution of sentence at the barrière du Trône. My maman would have wished me to do all I can to frustrate that."

"And so my mother would wish of me."

Mme Duclos had no answer.

"And the Canadian men?"

"At the conference, they said they had lived here for years in ease but, in all those years, they knew that they would one day be called to war. That day has come."

"So it is with me, aunt. The affair has nothing to do with civil government. I do not know whether France is better organised as a monarchy or as a republic, or governed by the Jacobin club or the Gironde. What matters is to disrupt – I dare not say prevent – a crime that will stain this city and this country for eternity. Against that, what is a carpenter's life?"

Mme Duclos said: "I have been summoned to the hôtel Brionne by the Committee of Security and Surveillance of the Convention. It seems that I have been denounced as being in treasonous correspondence with enemies of the Republic, meaning, I suppose, your father.

"I have not been in communication with your father.

"As you know, by reason of M. Duclos's service to the Congress in the late war, I am a citizen and pensioner of the States of America."

William did not know. He recognised that he knew very little of his aunt.

"I have asked Mr Morris, the delegate of the United States, to speak to the Committee on my behalf. Mr Morris has, it appears, more important business."

Mme Duclos smiled. "I am afraid I shall disappoint Sir James Stokes. M. Sanson, gentleman of Paris and executioner, has my name, dear William; and once he has dealt with me, he shall search for you. Let us die at a time and place of our choosing."

"Yes, aunt."

"We shall want powder."

"By good fortune, aunt, I have powder."

"And lead?"

"By God's mercy, Aunt Duclos, you have two acres of lead roof."

Mme Duclos had fallen into reverie.

"Whatever its virtues," Mme Duclos said, "popular government is always more vindictive than monarchy. And, young friend, these men and women are virtuous, and there is nothing more pitiless than virtue." Then: "Have you the cloth I gave you?"

William put his hand to his heart. He said: "It is with me always."

XXIII

William rose before dawn that 26th day of July 1794 (8 thermidor an 11) for he had a long tramp before him. He needed to traverse a great part of the eastern suburbs of the city of Paris, and this time not in burning aerostat, but on two bridge-builder's feet.

The invention of Dr Guillotine had, like all such advances in industrial technique, made possible an increase in volume. Originally erected before the Town Hall in the place de Grève, which was found too narrow for the horde of spectators, the scaffold was moved westward to the Carrousel, then each side of the broad place Louis XV, now known as the place de la Révolution. It was there that the King and Queen had lost their lives.

The tides of blood and the mass of men and women pouring in from the popular quarters to the east induced such disgust among the bourgeois in the west of town that the machine was moved back eastwards to place de la Bastille and then, on 25 prairial an II (June 13, 1794), to a

waste ground beyond the furthest edge of the faubourg
Saint-Antoine.

The ground was called the place du Trône, for there, back
in the great king's reign in the preceding century, thrones
had been set for Louis XIV and his new bride on their entry
into the city. It was an irregular amphitheatre, planted with
unhappy elm-trees, rising in the middle to what had once
been the base of a triumphal arch, never completed and now
demolished.

In newer times, the tax contractors, or farmers as they
were called, had built a barrier at the eastern entry to impose
dues on the animals, provisions, fire-wood and luxuries
brought in from the surrounding country. The place had been
renamed, without ingenuity, the barrière du Trône-renversé,
the throne in question having been over-turned. Beyond the
eastern barrier was an avenue of elms that led into the fields
and woods of the old royal hunting park of Vincennes. It was
as if the Parisians wished the apparatus to be expelled into
the wastes. William wondered if the Terrorists were being
driven even from the faubourg Saint-Antoine. He thought:
This blood-letting is coming to an end.

The barrier to the east was guarded by handsome star-
shaped sentry-boxes. Rising out of them were the stumps
of two columns, for which figures had not been supplied.
To the north and south were pavilions built for the business and convenience of the tax-collectors. Against the

southern pavilion, evident from the stench and the bloody sand strewed across the ground, was the scaffold covered by a tarpaulin.

The pavilions were deserted, the undertakers of the tax farm having either been done to death or escaped into exile. The park, planted by Louis XV with trees that had now reached a respectable height, was crossed by wide alleys scattered with market gardens. Beyond was the château de Vincennes, which the revolutionaries had sought, with small success, to demolish.

Bringing his small force in presented to William no great problem. The question was how to bring the good women and his band off the battle-field and out of Paris. There was not the smallest chance of getting away down the rue du faubourg Saint-Antoine westward into the city, or south to the bridge of Charenton.

At the south-east edge of the park, some two leagues distant, or six kilomètres as William was teaching himself to reckon, was the bridge of Saint-Maur. Here the Marne river, flowing down from the north-east, makes a great loop to the south, before returning to pour its tribute of fresh water into the Seine at Charenton. The peninsula enclosed by the loop of the river had been the site of the great Abbey of Saint-Maur. Much too good for mother church, the place had been taken (with the consent of the Holy Father) by a worldly bishop for his own use. Too good for him, it had passed to Catherine de Médicis and then to a cadet branch of the royal family, the ducs de Bourbon or Condé. Alarmed by the sacking of the castle of the Bastille, the dukes had that very month of July 1789 left the country. As with all the property of emigrants, the place was confiscated to the state. Many were the bourgeois in the west of town who cast envious eyes upon its stones, walks and acres.

Upstream of the neck of the peninsula was the bridge of Saint-Maur which carried the highway to Tournan and then on into Brie and, further east, to Nancy and Strasbourg. William had often crossed it. An old span of timber had been replaced, about seventy years before, by one of stone over seven arches. Its western end abutted the park of the château de Vincennes and the inns and cottages of the village of Saint-Maur-des-Fossés. Its central arch was set in a little riverine island, the île Fanac, dotted with woods, cottages and market gardens. The island seemed, to William's inspection, an excellent place to lay up a night.

Just a single cart's breadth, or a little over two metres in width, the bridge could be held by a force as exiguous as their own. Even a regiment of Guards would be reduced to just four files. Just as important, William saw with excitement, because of the loop in the Marne, any pursuers could approach only along the right or west bank of the river. His people would be quite safe from the rear. The parapets of the bridge, if built up with rubbish, would shield them from fire from the right bank.

Furthermore, any force from the place du Trône would have a greater distance to cover. It must needs traverse two sides of a triangle while his people, racing through the park of the château de Vincennes, would have the hypotenuse. William fought to suppress his elation. He wondered if God wished to give them *une chance en deux*, an even chance.

At the conference that evening, William said:

"We need a wagon and team. And we must take and hold the bridge of Saint-Maur until the good sisters are away."

There was silence. Then Ninnipen spoke:

"*Le canon anglais.*"

The English cannon.

"Is it sound?"

"*Nous verrons.*"

We shall see.

"*En double.*"

We must load double-shot.

Since dawn, at the furnace beneath the hot-wall at the foot of the garden, Ninnipen and the Canadians had been casting lead bullets and grape-shot.

It was resolved that William would command at the place du Trône, Ninnipen on the island, while Mme Duclos would bring up the cannon and chaises and speed the good sisters on their road.

XXIV

The barrier was guarded, but as William approached in the wagon from the park, the National Guardsmen opened the double gate. His passengers had the air of convicts, indeed were convicts, had been in prison tumbrils, some more than once, and knew how to conduct themselves. Ragged, filthy, stained with blood, some shouted defiance, others wept, a third part raised chained hands in pleas for compassion or mercy. They stood or rested against the wagon side-rails, waist deep in dirty straw; the which concealed their weapons and three wine barrels, two filled with black powder, the third with sand, all sealed, fused and numbered with chalk.

Ninnipen had selected the men from the company of indigenous felons. It seemed to William, as he drove the wagon through the barrier, that they had no special attachment to religion, far less female monasticism, but to a man and woman they wanted a fight: to break a piece of the world that had broken them. Even in the most desperate affairs, even at the forlorn station of the universe, a man believes that he may survive. As much to the point, all had been given money and, in the unlikely event of success, would receive more.

Never in his life had William seen such a crowd, but what astonished him, more than its numbers, was its stillness. Tobacco-smoke hung like shreds of mist in the hot air. There was no sound or movement, except from his left the whisper of women's voices singing psalms. From the scaffold, the blade of the killing-machine winked at William.

Below it, hemmed in by guardsmen, was the cart carrying the Carmelite sisters. Through the slats of the cart, he saw them, in their choir-mantles, confined like beasts at the door of the abattoir, hands tied behind backs, their wet habits filthy and stuck with straw, singing the Miserere. One of their number, old and crippled, was spreadeagled on the pavement, her crutches beyond her arms' reach.

William was overcome by savagery. He whispered: "You have come to see death, and you shall see death."

At the very crown of the place, William reined in the horses and, over his shoulder, gave his order. Two men stepped down without haste and lowered the cart back-board. The first barrel rolled out, match lit, and rumbled down the slope towards the rue du faubourg Saint-Antoine.

The crowd looked on as with a single pair of eyes. Some, no doubt, thought it was drink to wet the occasion. Then somebody, or many somebodies, saw the match and the place erupted. Like frightened cattle, they poured in a mass towards the gate of the faubourg. William sprang down and ran towards the women's tumbril. One of the guards raised his musket.

"Put that down, fool," William shouted, and then a blast of scalding air knocked him to the ground. Winded, he rose and saw, through billows of smoke and flying débris, that the guard were running and the scaffold deserted. The second barrel, filled only with earth but match lit, pursued the running guardsmen like an enraged bull. The wagon-horses, their eyes white with terror, were thrashing in their traces, the coachman frozen in place. The pavement was strewn with clothes and shoes and pieces of gleaming flesh. Everywhere were shrieks and sobs. The place smelled like a cook-house.

His men were carrying the crippled sister, crutches and all, to the cart. William kicked out the coachman, took the reins, climbed up onto the box, turned and said: "Mme de Thelles, we shall take you to safety."

A lady, bolt upright at the rear of the vehicle, said:

"We have chosen the path of martyrdom."

William saw that the women had gone deep into themselves, to a depth he could not begin to imagine; and the pain of surfacing was unendurable. Nothing in his life had prepared him for that.

Mme de Thelles said: "We have offered ourselves as a holocaust to appease God's anger and bring peace to the Church and to France."

William said: "Mother, God has found you worthy of suffering for Him and has returned you your lives."

The lady prepared to dispute the point. William took refuge in the rough soldier.

William said: "Mme de Thelles, you shall have opportunity enough to be martyred, on this very day."

"Quit your prosing," someone shouted from the second wagon. Spent musket balls were rattling about them. William cracked his whip and they were off, crunching over the horrors strewn on the ground.

The barrier was deserted. The other wagon halted, so that the men could drop the last barrel, lighten their load and destroy the powder. William passed them and whipped on, lest the blast reach them. Racing through the whispering trees, past foot-passengers with their mouths agape, and vehicles scuddering out of the way, William was exhilarated. So far, he thought, no loss.

Over his shoulder, William shouted: "Sing, brave ladies!"

Since there was no answer, William himself bawled: "*Te deum laudamus . . .*"

Then it came, in the voices of the living dead:

"*Te deum confitemur . . .*"

Thus singing away, they passed out of the park, through the houses at the bridge-head, and onto the bridge. With another surge of relief, William saw that M. Ninnipen and his people were in possession and waving them on between parapets built up with rubbish. In the middle was a dark shape covered with tarpaulin. At the far end of the bridge, William saw his aunt, dressed as a civil man in coat, hat and breeches. As they approached, she bowed low to the sisters. William reined in and jumped down. He hoped that Mme Duclos had a deeper store of casuistry to deploy with Mme de Thelles.

Ninnipen's men, when William joined them above the island, were standing at loop-holes in the barricade. The Huron gestured for silence.

On the far bank, a company of cavalry was coming up the quay from Charenton, all jingles and flashing steel, at hand-gallop. At the head, on a good animal, was a captain and just behind him two sergeants. Ninnipen had his hands clasped. Of a sudden, he spread them and William was unsighted by powder-smoke. As it cleared, he saw the troop in disorder, a riderless horse clattering towards them on the bridge, and two others careering into the troop. William had heard that the native men shot well, but not that well.

There are moments in a fight when a quick-witted soldier, seeing his officers fall, will himself take command. This was not such a moment. The cavalrymen, having seen their officers dropped by single shots at one hundred and fifteen yards, wheeled about and became horribly entangled.

Ninnipen had turned his head to the right. Beyond the gate of the park, above the trees, William could see dust; and then heard, sieved by the trees, broken shouts and snatches of what might have been "La Marseillaise". The cavalry troop was now in some sort of order, but could not put spur to flank, even if it were inclined to. A mob of dust and people was spilling out of the park.

"*C't à ton tour, Veelum.*"

It is your turn, William.

William stepped onto the crown of the bridge roadway, raised his hand, and beckoned the people to approach into ear-shot. They surged forward with a roar and then stopped on their heels. (Ninnipen had pulled the tarpaulin off the cannon. William could feel at his back the heat from the port-fire.) A distance of some eighty yards, or seventy metres, separated William from the crowd.

William spoke up. He said: "Citizens of the Republic of the French! The munition behind me is loaded with mitraille, in double charge." Pleasant to William was his voice in the sunshine, like wine or tobacco. "When I drop this right arm, the cannon shall be fired. The mitraille will convert me to atoms, and kill every one of you in the first twelve ranks. Yet, further back, one of you good people will be hit in the breast, another in the eye, a third in the kidneys, another in the reproductive organs. I think you would be wise to let the brave women depart. Then, if you wish to fight (which I do not advise), we shall fight."

William paused to allow the intelligence to be absorbed. Looking at the heads before him, William saw not a man or woman was listening. A murmur was making its way from the back.

There is nothing so irritating to a man as to make his peace with death and discover that nobody is attending.

There was a fellow before him with a butcher's knife. William addressed him:

"What has happened, citizen?"

"The Committee is dissolved. Citizen Robespierre is imprisoned. Citizen Saint-Just likewise."

William half turned and saw his Aunt Duclos. As he looked on her beloved shape, she shook down her carbine and, in a single movement, caught it, pulled it to her shoulder and fired. William felt the heat of the ball against his cheek. From behind him he heard a cry, the fall of a body and the clang of metal on the bridge pavement. The fellow must have wanted to use his blade while he was still able.

William turned to the people. Before him was only dust and a dead man.

He said: "Thank you, Aunt Duclos. You have saved my life."

"I put it in danger. It was the least I could do."

The Hurons were disabling the cannon.

"I see that you have not forgotten your riflewoman's exercises."

"I drill every Sunday. After Mass."

William said to the men, without thought: "Break the parapet. Tip the thing into the river."

So it was that a piece of heavy ordnance, cast by Bowen at Cowden on the Medway in the English county of Kent, fired twenty-six times at Fontenoy, lost at the second battle of Québec and spiked on the bridge of Saint-Maur, sank to the bed of the Marne river.

Wages were paid, and embraces exchanged; after which the insurgents dispersed, in twos and threes, some on foot, some in carts and chaises, to every point of the compass in the wide land of France.

XXV

The next morning, 10 thermidor an II, the Republic of France was in new hands. M. Robespierre, M. Saint-Just and their friends, and many others who were thought to be in the way, were slaughtered in the security of the place de la Révolution. The events at the place du Trône and on the Saint-Maur bridge became entangled in the general tumult.

It was said, on the authority of the last person to speak, that the liberation of the Carmelites had been staged by M. Robespierre's opponents to draw the attention of the people of Paris away from the revolt in the Convention and the Committee of Public Safety. Those who had preserved in secret their religious faith (and, particularly, many of the women of Paris) were certain that the sisters' prayers on the scaffold had been answered. They had witnessed a miracle of our times. The infidels saw a perfectly executed military manoeuvre, the two being identical.

The house at rue Varenne was shut up, one of the window-blinds on the upper floor of the *corps-de-logis* banging in the wind. Nobody remarked that the old English cannon had disappeared from the front court. The sisters were at the Carmelite house at Ávila in Spain, where they were revered as *las mártires vivientes* or the living martyrs. The Hurons were encamped in the woods of La Ferté-Joyeuse. William was with his people at Strasbourg. As quarter-master, he had to explain only to himself how he had lost two ton of powder. Mme Duclos was, as ever, out of sight. (She was attending as servant her friend Agnès Neiret aboard *L'Indomptable*, Captain Neiret commanding, on the Toulon station.)

In the Convention, the incident passed with knowing looks. In secret, all Paris was troubled at the new force in the affairs of the Republic: mysterious, pitiless, of small number, expert; without policy, publicity or champions. Ever alert for English plots, the Jacobins wondered if the scheme had been hatched across the Channel by that devil Milord Stokes. But why should that man, or any man, care for nuns?

There was a suspicion that M. Fouché, deputy of the department of Loire-inférieure, was in the secret, but that citizen always gave that impression. When questioned directly, Citizen Fouché shook his head in what appeared to be regret, turned and walked away. Was he mourning the death of Maximilien de Robespierre or the escape of the fanatic women? Had he premonition of the fall of the Republic? One of the National Guardsmen on the bridge had reckoned the cannon to be of English manufacture. Yet to haul the piece out of the river would merely resurrect the incident.

In the midst of the disorder, on August 31st, 1794, a Sunday, at a quarter past seven in the morning, the Poudrerie at the château de Grenelle blew up. A spark from La Liberté graining-mill ignited sixty-five thousand pounds of black powder. Five hundred workmen, guards, women and servants, and all sixty horses in the stables, were killed in half a second. A further five hundred persons died of their injuries on tumbrils or at the hospitals.

The blast broke every window in the Military College, the hospital of the Invalides and the hôtels in the rue Varenne. The records of the factory, including accounts of all the tonnage consigned to the army since mid-summer, were burned or dispersed by the winds. M. Chaptal, who had been out shooting game the day previous in the park of Bercy and returned at midnight, had lain in his bed at the hôtel of the administration, quai Malaquai, and was saved. He was fortunate in that M. Robespierre was no more. The chemist's absence on that terrible morning, for the first time in four months, would have condemned him without hearing to the guillotine. In the new dispensation after Thermidor, chemistry was of greater service to the nation than virtue. A week later, fire broke out in the saltpetre refinery at the former Abbey of Saint-Germain-des-Prés.

Amid those alarms, the fate of the Carmelite sisters, the massacre in the place du Trône and the tussle at the Saint-Maur bridge were placed in a dossier and locked away.

Only two men in all Europe understood.

The first was M. de Buonaparte. He alone, of the whole artillery service of the French Republic, had seen an English cannon in the outer court of the hôtel Joyeuse-Neilson. On 14 vendémiaire an III (October 6th, 1795), the day after he had cannonaded a Royalist demonstration outside the church of Saint-Roch, rue Saint-Honoré, Brigadier General Buonaparte had his coachman stop at the house in rue Varenne. An old soldier opened the gate. A torn tricolore waved from a staff above the *corps-de-logis*, where the upper windows were still without glass from the explosion at the powder factory at the château de Grenelle. Parts of the lead roof had been torn off and not replaced. The outer court was empty but for a woman hanging out washing.

The porter came out with his boots unlaced.

M. Buonaparte said: "Where is the cannon that was here, good friend?"

"Citizen Neilson sent the piece to the army. We heard it did mighty execution at Valmy."

The officer laughed and gave the man a crown. Naturally forgiving, and now the saviour of the Revolution, M. Buonaparte wondered what had become of William Neilson. Emigrated, for certain.

The other gentleman was Mr Godfrey. He, too, under another name, had seen the English six-pounder in the courtyard of his beloved's house. He wished that the lady had permitted the Carmelite saints to be martyred. He thought: M. Fouché will dredge the Marne, raise the cannon and find his way to Canada and Mme Duclos.

XXVI

When Gnaeus Pompey became too beloved of the Roman public for the taste of the Roman Senate, those magistrates despatched him, in the year 67 B.C., to the eastern Mediterranean, in part to quell piracy and, in part, so he might come to harm. Determined, as ever, to relive the history of the Roman Republic, the Thermidoreans, assembled in a committee called the Directory, proposed in 1797 that General Buonaparte go and conquer Egypt. He could then, if accident had not befallen him, proceed eastwards and eject the English from India.

That officer, eager to indulge his taste for geography and ancient history, and (at certain moments) to emulate

Alexander of Macedon, readily agreed. Amid an army of forty thousand, ten thousand sailors and many score of savants, mathematicians, naturalists, botanists, chemists, engineers and scholars of Arabic and hieroglyphs, General Buonaparte carried across the Mediterranean but a single company of bridge-makers, with a strength of seventy-five men, among them Lieutenant Niellon.

William could not forget the place du Trône. Even as he supervised the debarcation of horses at Alexandria, he had in his ears the blast of the barrel and the shrieking of the crippled men and women. The shock of battle had receded, leaving a shame that stopped him dead. He attempted, in daylight, to take a worldly view. If, William reasoned, you set out to enjoy the spectacle of harmless women dying in filth and agony, you must accept a risk of injury to yourself; else the pastime is not, as the English have it, "sport". Such urbanity was alien to his nature. His nights were torment. The seventeen men, women and children he had killed passed in review.

How far must you fall before you touch ground?

William was at Damietta, at Cairo and Gizeh, and at the siege of Acre in 1799. General Buonaparte, who disliked lumber on the march, had brought no siege-train and a flotilla of heavy guns despatched from Alexandria was captured by Captain Sir Sydney Smith of the Royal Navy. William proposed that his men attempt to bring off two howitzers from an English chaloupe that had foundered in the road. Having swum out in the warm sea and dismantled the guns, and unarmed but for their implements, they were easily taken by marines from H.M.S. *Theseus*. Expecting to be exchanged, they were handed over to the Turkish governor of the town and confined in the citadel. Two weeks later, they were told that General Buonaparte had abandoned the siege, and the army marched back to Cairo.

From his turnkeys, William learned not only the Arabic language spoken in Syria and Palestine but something of the philosophy of the Muslims. He saw that his captors had not the smallest interest in Equality and Fraternity, for their religion gave them both; and, as for Liberty, the laws of Islam gave them all the freedom they required and anything beyond that was libertinage, sin or innovation.

One day, while directing the repair of one of the land-side bastions of the city wall, William was questioned by the gaolers as to why Frenchmen prostituted their wives and daughters. He replied that the French ladies were so virtuous that they were granted more latitude than was usual in other nations. William's response, though self-evidently false and wicked, was too much for his inquisitors and they retired to recover their formation.

In gaol, time is like a river, where quick runs are followed by slow and placid reaches. It must have been much later, for the prisoners were working on the sea-side wall, that Yousef Bey sidled up and asked: "You are an educated man, Mousa Wil. Tell us, is Jesus son of God? Or is God son of Jesus? Would you kindly explain?"

William put down his chalk and slate and took a step back.

He answered: "Gentlemen, had I uttered such a blasphemy, you would, with justice, have hanged me from that bretesche. I cannot answer, lest I, too, fall into blasphemy."

Once again, the Inquisition had to retreat and reform. The gaolers recognised that, if the theological debate were to proceed, it was necessary to have their disputant in full possession of his reasoning. Rations improved; and since the cookery in that part of the globe is excellent, William and his men gained in health and strength. There were no more beatings on the soles of the feet or blows to the kidneys. Sometimes, they were given tangled snippets of news. Their general had, it seemed, conquered Italy and was now Sultan of France.

William found much to interest him in the ancient city, with its mementoes of the Crusades, of Saladin and King Philip of France and of Richard of England and Normandy. The ancient walls that had seen so many sieges made admirable quarries for his repairs.

On 6 messidor an X (June 25th, 1802), a definitive treaty of peace was signed at Paris between Citizen Talleyrand, on behalf of First Consul Buonaparte of France, and Sayyid

Ghalib Effendi, foreign secretary to the sublime Ottoman Sultan. The Eighth Article of the treaty affirmed that should there be any prisoners, detained as a consequence of war, they should immediately be freed without ransom. William's gaolers, in tears, begged them to remain.

A Russian warship carried the prisoners, less four men who had become Muslims, married and settled in Palestine, to Ajaccio, whence they made their way to Marseille. From shipboard William saw the white city swing into view under the sails, and a pair of verses from the school-room at La Brienne came unbidden into his consciousness:

Heureux qui, comme Ulysse, a fait un beau voyage
Ou comme cestuy-là qui conquit la toison

Happy the man that, like Ulysses, has made a fair voyage

Or like that Jason-chap, who captured the Golden Fleece

A quarantine on the blinding island of Pomègues, with no shade but a canvas awning and only hot brine to drink, drove the couplet, and all lyric verse, out of our friend's head.

William's men, reduced by two more by the amenities of the port city, regained Strasbourg and received a less than heart-felt welcome. They had been listed as fallen in action and their duties and privileges assigned to others; and it took some doing on William's part to convince the officers that they were alive and eager once again to serve the Republic.

XXVII

Mr Godfrey's counterpart in Paris, or *homologue*, as we say, was M. Fouché, Minister of General Police at Paris.

Born in the west country into a family active in the trade in African slaves, as a lad M. Joseph Fouché had been sent to the Oratory at Nantes where he matriculated devout and graduated atheist and Freemason. A delegate to the Convention, at the outbreak of war, M. Fouché was sent to quell the uprisings in the Vendée and Lyon, where his brutality disgusted even M. Robespierre. What role he played in that gentleman's fall on 8 thermidor was not at all clear to Mr Godfrey. Mr Godfrey wished, not for the first time, that he had defied King George and, as some clownish *enragé* from the fields in clogs and cockades, attended the Convention, taken part in debates and observed across the floor of the Salle des Machines the principal personalities of revolutionary France.

Under the Directory, M. Fouché put some fat on his ribs as a contractor or *munitionnaire* for the armies in the Low Countries. A little later, he was French minister at The Hague, where Mr Godfrey, under some disguise or other, took the trouble to study him.

M. Fouché seemed to Mr Godfrey to have no weaknesses. He liked money, but not too much. Women, likewise. He disliked God, but not to death. He seemed to our friend to have no beliefs, only a sense of order. Like certain ingenious animals and reptiles, M. Fouché took his colour from his surroundings.

Together with M. Buonaparte's brothers, he strewed sand in the way of that officer's rise to power on the famous 18 brumaire an VIII (November 9th, 1799). As a conspirator, M. Fouché was never at the front, but always at the rear, so he could see men's backs and none could see his. Now First Consul, M. Buonaparte reckoned only M. Fouché could keep in check the Jacobins and discipline those who, like children with a new spinning-top, wished for the revolution to go on and on and on. Only M. Fouché read all the inconvenient pamphlets and placards, was in the counsels of the Royalists, knew who was hoarding grain, who was demolishing churches, convents and castles for his or her own profit, could follow Prussian and English agents, controlled the post-houses and hireling stables. Only he could skim the gaming tables and disorderly houses of the capital and provincial cities to keep Mme Buonaparte in funds, while her husband won glorious victories in Italy.

Public girls, in order to pursue their commerce, must share with the police not only intelligence on their lovers but also their wage. The pecuniary produce is known in France as *la curée*. The phrase, which denoted in feudal times the skin of a game beast thrown as reward to hounds, had come to mean, in the city of Paris where sport is exercised

in-doors, the share due to the police from gaming and pros-
titution. Mr Godfrey computed that it was yielding to
M. Fouché a million francs each day. Much of that went to
pay the expenses of M. Buonaparte's all but limitless family,
but still left Citizen-minister Fouché with resources incom-
parably greater than those of the foreign letter office and its
secretary.

Unlike M. Robespierre, M. Buonaparte had no objec-
tion to nobility, only wished (like most men) that the order
be re-constituted with his mother at the pinnacle. For
those who feared a restoration of the royal government,
M. Fouché was consolation: the lone survivor of the revolutionary years, the only regicide still in affairs, the man
who had watched with dry eyes the Queen of France with
her own hands mend her stockings and shoes in preparation for the gallows, the fighting rear-guard of a failed
republic. Citizen-minister Fouché's very existence was also
guarantee to those high military officers who owed their
rise to the revolution and to the new rich who had bought
at forced sales the emigrants' lands or, like M. Ballin, son
of old Mme Neilson's intendant at La Ferté-Joyeuse,
demolished the Abbey of Les Thelles and sold the stones
for his own account, that they would preserve their places
and emoluments.

Mr Godfrey and M. Fouché conversed, but not in words.
A dead courier in Turin, the violation of a nun in Tarragona,

a burned transport in Valletta harbour were what for us are pleasantries, like talk of the weather or the harvest. Each knew the other inside out.

Mr Godfrey knew his adversary was unprincipled, treacherous and distrusted by the Emperor.

M. Fouché, in turn, did not for an instant believe that Sir James Stokes was breeding milk-cows in the Principality of Wales. Why would any man want to do that? He did not know that Mr Godfrey and Sir James Stokes were one and the same. He did know, from the chatter of penitent Royalists, that Sir James as Ambassador Plenipotentiary had loved a woman of Paris and so, by deduction, must his present avatar. It was a matter of finding that woman and turning her and her lover to his purposes.

Where was the bitch?

Mr Godfrey knew that the First Consul was frightened of M. Fouché and that, at some point, when he felt safe, he would dispense with his Minister of Police. Mr Godfrey knew that he must do nothing to bring Mme Duclos to safety, and that he must trust her with his life, as she trusted him with hers. At times, he entertained a fugitive wish that, when the war was over, if the war were ever over, they would live together in Canada in the most complete seclusion. At better moments, he knew that they were so bound together that they might verily be man and wife.

XXVIII

The massacre in the place du Trône-renversé had by no means been forgotten. In particular, young William's use of fused iron-bound powder-barrels in a vehicle intrigued some men of an experimental bent, both Jacobin and Royalist. In the night of October 17th–18th, 1800, there was a violent explosion in the waste ground beyond the hospital of La Salpetrière on the south-east edge of Paris. From the gazettes and the word of travellers, Mr Godfrey knew that the whole city was on edge.

On the night of Christmas Eve, 1800 (3 nivôse an IX), the First Consul, Mme Buonaparte and other members of the family set off from the Tuileries in two coaches to attend a performance of the oratorio *La Création*, by Haydn, at the Salle Montansier, rue de Richelieu. In the rue Saint-Nicaise, at the point where it debouches into rue Saint-Honoré, the First Consul's carriage sped past a stopped wagon, its horses held by a young girl. As the coach with the ladies approached, the wagon exploded, killing the girl and seven persons, knocking Mme Buonaparte senseless and wounding the arm of her daughter by her first marriage, Hortense de Beauharnais. None the less, the whole family proceeded to the concert. The First Consul had inherited, it appears, something of Caesar's luck.

Many thought that M. Fouché would be pensioned, or

worse, but the diligent citizen-minister assembled some Bretons who confessed, under some duress, that they had received money from Sir James Stokes in England to carry out the plot. Only Mr Godfrey knew that to be untrue and he wondered if the First Consul was persuaded. The assassination in Saint Petersburg of Tsar Paul the following March, garrotted in his bedroom by drunken Guardsmen, could not have added to the First Consul's feelings of security.

Mr Godfrey imagined the scene at the Tuileries or Saint-Cloud. As the gentlemen leave his cabinet, the First Consul calls Citizen-minister Fouché to remain a moment. M. Fouché turns back and the door is closed behind him.

"Citizen-minister, will you find Neilson for me?"

M. Fouché has an expression that displays neither knowledge nor ignorance.

"Yes, sir."

"Neilson was my school-mate at Brienne and at the Military College. I suppose he is with the emigrants. Will you tell him that he shall be received with honour? And that his property shall be restored?"

"Yes, sir."

Then, returning to his writing-desk, M. Buonaparte says: "I did him a bad turn, once, which weighs on my conscience."

If M. Fouché has a fault, it is a reluctance to credit a generous impulse.

The names of the *émigrés* were listed, with that French precision that had slid down intact from the Old Régime, in nine heavy volumes. Originally comprising some one hundred and fifty thousand men and women, their numbers had by death or pardon been reduced to just over half, or eighty-five thousand. No Neilson was found. Alas, M. Fouché did not know that the Gaelic patronymic prefix *Mac-* was identical to the Scots and English suffix *-son*.

Did M. Fouché search for young William in the army lists? Did he know that written texts are corrupted in transmission? Out of ignorance, haste, prejudice or intention, copyists will often reduce unfamiliar words to the familiar of their time and place. Was M. Fouché schooled in the editorial principle known to savants as *difficilior lectio*? Always prefer the more abstruse of the readings: Neilson not Niellon.

Such are the workings of Fortune. Had William accepted Count Bielke's challenge and survived the exchange of shots or, rather, had he not resigned his commission, he might have risen on his capacities to a high rank, or, like Davoust, who was two classes below him at the Military College, have earned fame as a commanding general. M. Fouché did not think to search for a laborious lieutenant of bridge-makers. William did not know what I know: that Count Bielke, in taking his happiness, had given him his life.

XXIX

The First Consul's victories in Italy had not only added to his lustre and expanded French dominion, they had opened new territory for Mr Godfrey's operations. The cost of his troop of *confidenti*, or informants, in Italy and Spain could not be borne under the old revenue system. By good fortune, Mr Shelby had been rewarded by Mr Pitt's Ministry with a Lordship of Treasury, where his habits of profligacy, developed at the tables in White's Club, proved of service to the foreign letter office.

For some time, the interceptions had revealed some broadening in the French Republic's religious sentiments. On 18 thermidor an IX (August 6th, 1801), M. Fouché issued an instruction to journalists to cease to use the language of 'Ninety-three about the clergy and, instead, make no reference whatsoever to religion. A little later, priests that had gathered at the Spanish frontier were permitted to return, provided only they took an oath to the Republican constitution. The First Consul appointed three men, including a clerical gentleman, to arrange with the Holy See a restoration of the Roman Catholic cult in the French Republic and its territories. In one of those whims that come to official men of a certain age, Mr Godfrey thought it prudent to have his own delegate at the Conference.

What caused our friend one night to leave the General

Post Office by the alley and board at Deptford the fighting sloop H.M.S. *Ariadne* bound for the Ionian Islands, was this. His agent at the Conference, Cardinal F—, had written (in a Latin of which Cicero might have been proud) that the French delegates had offered, without prejudice but as a gesture of good sentiment towards the Holy See, to receive the Carmelite sisters of Les Thelles back in their homeland.

Mr Godfrey alighted at Corfu and proceeded, in a Venetian bottom, to the lagoon city. In his years as a merchant-banker, Mr Godfrey had done much business at Venice, but he found the place sad, the churches stripped by the French armies or turned into barracks or timber-stores, the Lion of Saint Mark taken from his pillar by the Mole and a void where the gold horses of Byzantium had reared their golden hooves above the basilica. Having denuded the place of its treasures, the First Consul, with his usual open-handedness, had given the city and parts of its hinterland to Austria.

Mr Godfrey did not long remain to mourn the alterations. Soon after his departure, by post-chaise, over the Brenner to Innsbruck, an article appeared in the foreign pages of the *Notizie del mondo* under the heading "The Living Martyrs!" In it, the author, who signed himself "Fidelis" or Faithful, rejoiced in the imminent return to France of the Carmelite sisters and the re-construction, at the expense of the state, of their house at Les Thelles. Could this be harbinger, Fidelis asked his readers, of the Restoration of the Holy Church in that unhappy land and, even, *sotto voce*, of Royalty?

A second article, in which Mr Godfrey covered the same ground but, as it were, from the contrary direction, was printed three days later, under the title "Reaction in France", in the *Gazzetta di Parma*. The author, who this time signed himself "Brutus", asked: Was Liberty to be sacrificed for a few worn-out nuns? Was Equality to give way to the mutterings of disconsolate women in freezing chapel choirs? Was ecclesiastical property, converted since the Revolution to productive purposes, to be once again so much dead weight upon the Earth? Was First Consul Buonaparte become a second General Monck, he who betrayed the English revolution in 1660 and, for a paltry dukedom, brought back the clottish Stuart Kings? (The last sentence was, Mr Godfrey later reckoned, asking too much of his readers.)

In intelligencing, there is rarely a sure chain of cause and effect. Mr Godfrey noted that neither in the text of the agreement or Concordat signed at the Tuileries by Joseph Bonaparte and Cardinal Consalvi on 26 messidor an IX (July 15th, 1801), nor, as far as he could tell, in any secret annexe to the treaty, was there mention of restoration in France of Catholic monasticism, whether male or female.

XXX

The war had exhausted both France and England. Like blood-
ied prize-fighters, neither could land a telling blow. Britain's
allies on the continent were licked, the Pitt government had
fallen and the Whigs in Parliament and manufacturers in the
towns were baying for peace. The First Consul wished to make
improvements to the civil government of France and the conquered territories, and to recover Saint-Domingue from the
blacks who, believing that Liberty, Equality and Fraternity
comprised them also, had taken command of the island. The
peace, signed at Amiens that March of 1802, was greeted with
delight.

While others frolicked, the letter office in London and
the Ministry of Police at Paris were, like shop-keepers at
Christmas, overwhelmed with business. Amid the flocks of
thoughtless English noblemen and -women alighting in
Paris, M. Fouché had every expectation that Sir James Stokes
would come in person to have news of his mistress. Mr Godfrey stayed at home. He had quite as much work attending
the travellers in Bordeaux and Burgundy wines, minutely
inspecting the ports and fortifications of Harwich, Plymouth
and Portsmouth.

He knew the First Consul was a reader of newspapers,
and susceptible to flattery. With his own hand, Mr Godfrey
wrote articles for *Le courrier de Londres* that were Royalist in

tenor, but not Bourbonnist. France, Mr Godfrey wrote, would ever be a monarchy and in the Corsican soldier she had a man worthy of the throne of Charlemagne.

Rather as one lifts one's whip in the run-in of a steeple-chase, M. Fouché sent an Irishman to Stockholm. The visitor told His Britannic Majesty's envoy in that city that he had intelligence of great motions in the west of Ireland but would convey that only to Sir James Stokes. Now, all those with knowledge of secret work are at one on this: what you desire, above all, to hear by way of intelligence is always and eternally false. In the town of Aachen or Aix-la-Chapelle, at the appointed time, Sir James took station not in his rooms at the Redoute but in the coffee-house on the other side of the Allee, where he was taking a loaf of rye bread, a polder cheese and a glass of Burgundy, no less.

"May I trouble you for a second glass, madame?"

The lady tutted at the extravagance, and bent beneath the counter to retrieve the precious liquid. Mr Godfrey took off his spectacles and turned his back to the window. The shock from the explosion blew out the store-glass. Poor fellow, Mr Godfrey thought as he helped his hostess to her feet, our friend never told him that the explosive charge was for two.

In contrast to M. Fouché, Mr Godfrey wanted his antagonist alive. At sixty-four years of age, the Englishman did not feel he could adjust his policy to the apprentice blunders and peculiarities of a new man, or the wild schemes of ambitious office-seekers. On some mornings, he felt too weary to stand up. The lines of intercepted writing swam before his eyes.

M. Fouché spared him much trouble and expense. Mr Godfrey did not need to circulate in Paris seditious journals, or paste Royalist declarations on alley-walls, for M. Fouché did that for him. It was not necessary for Mr Godfrey to make conspiracies, or send men to stir up the Vendée or the Chouans of Brittany, or demoralise the ship-yards of Brest and Toulon, for M. Fouché was much the more competent in such operations. Mr Godfrey knew that the Minister of Police, to preserve his office and his life, needed to keep the First Consul perpetually on edge.

Then Mr Covington made a mistake.

In a régime of absolute government, if you wish to injure a rival, you do not demean him. You praise him to the clouds. In the Palace of Westminster, against the door of the Commons chamber, and sometimes invading that sanctum, is a place called the Lobby, for ever infested with persons on business, servants, foot-men, chair-men, French spies, news-writers, pick-pockets, gallant women, bishops and peers. One day, in the usual tumult, Mr Covington was in good voice. Buonaparte is an exceptional fighting soldier, he said to a pair of auditors, and a commander who might stand comparison with Alexander and Caesar.

There was a drift towards the parliamentarian. "Alas," Mr

Covington said to the multiplying throng, "the First Consul has no gift for home affairs. But for M. Fouché, France would be in chaos and insurrection. In foreign relations, he would be helpless without M. Talleyrand, unfrocked Bishop of Autun." (In such matters, two names are better than one.) "If those gentlemen go, then all Buonaparte's victories in the field will count for nothing."

One did not need to drag the interceptions to suspect that the First Consul was infuriated. On 28 fructidor an X (September 15th, 1802), M. Fouché was raised to the toga of the Senate and the Ministry of General Police abolished. Generous as ever, and as rich from his conquests as any king of France since Clovis, the First Consul permitted the diligent citizen-minister to retain half the *curée* stacked in the cellars of the ministry, amounting to 2,400,000 francs and rising daily. M. Fouché now had the leisure and the funds to attend to his small estate at Pont-Carré, in pleasant wooded country to the east of the capital.

Mr Godfrey was not deceived. He thought that M. Fouché, like many men who have become inured to power in the state, could not live without it. To return to favour, M. Fouché needed to find the link between the place du Trône and the "infernal machine" that all but killed the First Consul and his family in the rue Saint-Nicaise. M. Fouché would not rest until he had brought to the Tuileries Sir James Stokes' head on a charger.

XXXI

One of the curiosities of the revolutionary governments in France was that they hoarded paper. By the decree of 7 messidor an II (June 25th, 1794), the principal records of the royal regime were to be (with exceptions) preserved and open to the public. M. Fouché pored over every item intercepted and copied or detached from the period of Sir James Stokes' Embassy in Paris.

As if in a mirror, the same was happening in London. Mr Tappin took on the duty of rifling the boxes from the old Northern Department, and quizzing every secretary and clerk on their communications in those years 1785–92. The work was both heavy and delicate, like laying a hedge to enclose live-stock. Mr Tappin had started to have ideas and, one day, taking the air in the alley, Mr Tappin had one of his best.

There had been but one married man at the Paris Embassy, Sir James' chaplain, M. Le Couteur. The reverend youth's bride had remained on the island of Guernsey, because she was expectant of their first child. M. Le Couteur devoted much of his time, in company with two doctors of the Sorbonne, to plotting the amalgamation of the Anglican and Gallican churches.

It was known in Sir James' house that M. Le Couteur wrote his wife each day at evening, not by the courier, but by the Post, and in French. The gentleman was now vicar at the ancient church of St Sampson on the island. Without informing his chief, Mr Tappin set off for the Bailiwick of Guernsey. After kicking his heels for some time in Southampton, Mr Tappin heard of a trader in grain in Brixham in Devonshire, and duly took passage.

The vicarage was a plain house hard by a funny old church, with a view across the harbour to the island of Herm.

Mme Le Couteur herself opened the door. She was a pretty young woman, with three children in the folds of her skirts. Mr Tappin introduced himself as a colleague of her husband from Paris days.

"M. Le Couteur is taking Sunday School."

"Then, madame, I shall take a turn about the harbour and return in an hour."

"Oh no, don't trouble yourself, sir. Come into the parlour."

Mme Le Couteur seemed to appreciate the unexpected company. Likewise the children, who emerged in ones and twos from the wainscoting, like house-mice at midnight. They showed the visitor, first with diffidence and then insistence, their drawings, silhouettes and prayer-samplers; and then such profane items as wagtails' nests, ammonites and thunderstones. It appeared that, in this remote place, there was a certain monotony that a guest from London, no less, might vary. The children may have sensed a loosening of the Sabbath rule.

Standing apart in the corner, all but asleep, was the most amiable creature Mr Tappin had ever encountered. It was a little girl shaped somewhat like a hen's egg: round about the middle and pointed at both top and bottom. Like some miraculous relic in a cathedral treasury, her Sunday pinafore preserved every trace of its bearer's activity.

Mme Le Couteur sat down, picked up her work and asked: "What news of Sir James?"

They had fallen into French.

"I have heard Sir James devotes himself to rural improvements. People speak of extraordinary advances."

"And the Grey Lady?"

Mr Tappin felt weary. He thought: Fouché will have her, and the Stone-thrower. There is nothing we can do for them. And Mr Godfrey can no longer read without a magnifying glass, and each day he is thinner than the day before. When he is gone, whichever man comes in for him, if any man comes in, that man will not care for two French private citizens of no political or military value.

From the church across the square, a din of cries and scraping chairs broke the Sunday silence.

"If you please, madame?"

"Mme Dubois, is it? Something like that. M. Le Couteur wrote to me of the lady's visit."

Mme Le Couteur's eyes flickered to a drawer at the base of her work-box.

At that moment, the Rev. M. Le Couteur stepped in. Mr Tappin stood.

"Tappin, dear fellow! What a surprise! And pleasure!"

M. Le Couteur took station by the fire-place. "And how is good Sir James?"

"Tending his cows in Wales."

"Shamefully treated! Shamefully."

Mr Tappin did not answer. He needed to press on.

"Forgive me, John, Mme le Couteur. I had a question that only you can answer."

"Can we do the mud fort?"

Invasion fever had reached the vicarage nursery.

"On the Sabbath Day! Of course not. Have you done your Sunday Questions?"

"Ye-e-e-e-s." Meaning, Mr Tappin supposed, No.

"Mud fort," The Egg murmured; and again, lest any doubt her command of the phrase, "Mud fort."

"O, very well," said M. Le Couteur.

There was a clatter of feet and slamming of doors.

"May I assure you, madame, and dear John, that I would not have so intruded but for pressing reasons of state? I need to see your correspondence from the time of Sir James' Embassy at Paris."

Mme Le Couteur pouted. M. Le Couteur said: "Surely, Timothy, you cannot wish to read the cooings of new marrieds."

"I shall not read the letters. I wish only to see the covers."

Mme Le Couteur reached down to her work-box, opened a drawer at the bottom, brought out a sheaf of letters and untied the ribbon that bound them. Without rising from her chair, but showing no firmer sign of displeasure, Mme Le Couteur held them out to our friend.

Mr Tappin made a fan of the letters. All had been opened and resealed. All had been copied. The work was not well done. Mr Silva would have wept.

Our friend needed to cover his tracks and reassure his hosts. The children had trickled back, for the fort could wait, but the interesting visitor might not.

"By your candour and kindness, you have done the Lords Secretary a great service."

"Is anything amiss, Timothy?"

"On the contrary, John."

"Will you not take a collation with us, M. Tappin?"

"On the thumb, as we say?"

"Alas, I am a prisoner of my captain who is eager to sail. I have time only," Mr Tappin said, rising and turning to the children, "TO INSPECT THE MUD FORT!"

The room emptied in shrieks.

The fort had been erected at the foot of a cliff, where a deep band of clay offered ample building material. The children had commenced with the outworks which, so it seemed to Mr Tappin, had been a mistake. One ravelin was complete and a second traced so as to furnish overlapping arcs of cross-fire. They determined to complete it that very evening. Tom and Gilles, the older boys from the Sunday School, were under Mr Tappin's orders, while the younger children were appointed scouts and sentries. One little fellow was digging a well, always of critical importance in a prolonged siege. The Egg had fallen into sleep, fanned by her sisters with mare's-tail ferns.

Mr Tappin sensed that the two lads knew they were being examined. He thought: It has no purpose. There will be no letter office once Mr Godfrey is out of business. Laborious, solitary, obscure, inglorious, unsafe and ill-rewarded, ours is no sort of life for these clever lads, with their steady hands and native French. Better that the boys don scarlet tunics and epaulettes. At least the girls of England will give them a second glance.

The next time he looked up, it was twilight, the tide was on the turn and the children, even Tom and Gilles, had slipped away for their bread-and-butter and their prayers. Without assistance, the visitor completed the ravelin.

As he walked by starlight the track to Saint-Peter's-Port, Mr Tappin found that his gloom had dispersed. He discovered, to his astonishment, that this Anglican idyll had given him the most intense happiness: the *densest* happiness he had known as an adult and, perhaps, as a child. It occurred to him, again perhaps, that one should not seek happiness for it will come, even to a drudge, at rare and precious moments and lighten one's way like the moon behind the benighted traveller.

He found the ship's company in the worst of moods. The anchor had fouled (or somesuch, Tim Tappin being no mariner) and they must wait on daylight. Mr Tappin found himself a corner of the inn, bespoke brandy and water, wrapped himself in his coat, and waited for the sun.

XXXII

Had Mr Tappin but known it, Mme Duclos was, at that moment, not fifty nautical miles away, in the hamlet of Diélette in Normandy, lodging with her widowed friend, Mme Neiret.

Captain Neiret, for all his forty years as a fighting sailor and eighteen prizes, including a Royal Navy First Rate, had succeeded in accumulating not one sou of ready money. His widow survived for a time on his naval pension, but it was paid in revolutionary paper that had lost all value, and then was not paid at all.

Mme Duclos was quite as poor as her friend. Mme Duclos had not set foot in Paris, or had any communication with her bankers, since the affair of the place du Trône. The ladies lived from the produce of their garden and the milk and butter from their good Cotentin cow. While M. Buonaparte crowned himself Emperor of the French and King of Italy, abolished the revolutionary calendar and recalled M. Fouché to his old duties, the friends took in sailors' washing for cash and mended fishermen's nets.

In a well-policed state, such as France under First Consul Buonaparte and now Emperor, it is not easy to hide. One must sit quite still in one place. One must take no action that might bring ink in conjunction with paper. One must not travel, marry, fall ill, give birth, borrow, steal, lend, rent, let, donate, endow, inherit, enlist. Above all, one must not die.

One day in 1804, Mmes Neiret and Duclos heard that two gentlemen had arrived by coach and were lodging at the inn "for some time". From the upper room, Mme Duclos espied through M. Neiret's glass a man-of-war with her boats lowered. As relict of the hero Captain Neiret, Agnès Neiret was, even by M. Fouché, untouchable. Mme Duclos kissed her friend and, with nothing but the dress, hat and shoes she had on her, walked out into the miry lane.

Mme Duclos believed that she must go back into her history and forget everything she had done or learned since first coming, as a child kitchen-maid, into the service of Mme Neilson in the year 1746. She must roll up her life and cut off every thread that M. Fouché might find and ravel. Mme Duclos walked into Brittany. She exchanged her clothes, bonnet and shoes for a skirt of fustian, sabots and a woollen shawl. She chipped her finger-nails on stones and rolled sticks in her palms till blisters formed and burst.

On the moors above the city of Brest, Mme Duclos took service with a farmer whose signal virtue was that he could neither read nor write. Mme Duclos washed floors, killed chickens, gelded pigs, skinned lambs. She became dirty, idle and shrill. She spread tales. She missed Isabelle, fit to weep.

She knew that in this wild place she was protecting Sir James Stokes, and young William. Her death would do as well or better.

Unusually for a servant-of-all-work in that department of the French Republic, Mme Duclos had read Arrian's *Discourses of Epictetus*. In the sluttish kitchen at dawn, as she blew the fire to life, Mme Duclos said to herself:

"καπνὸν πεποίηκεν ἐν τῷ οἰκήματι; ἂν μέτριον, μενῶ: ἂν λίαν πολύν, ἐξέρχομαι. τούτου γὰρ μεμνῆσθαι καὶ κρατεῖν, ὅτι ἡ θύρα ἤνοικται."

Does the chimney smoke? If only moderately, I shall stay. Too much and I shall leave. Remember this and hold it firm: the door is open.

Mme Duclos laughed.

"What are you so pleased about, slut?"

"Marguerite pissed in the pail."

That was, precisely, the style of pleasantry that M. Kirouac appreciated. He rose and drained the milk-can. He opened his mouth and white froth gushed down his beard and onto his shirt.

"Go to your work, bitch!"

Each day, for precisely an hour, at milking or pulling down the hay, Mme Duclos looked through the barn door down to the high road and counted the vehicles. One day, she saw a marching company of men. Mme Duclos walked out of the kitchen, leaving the door open.

Mme Duclos had preserved, in a corner of her mind, the thought that, when all else failed, she would make her way to the Convent of Saint-Joseph at Ávila and seek the protection of Mme de Thelles. She came down to Bayonne and crossed into Spain but, somewhere in the mountains in the vicinity of León, Mme Duclos lost her road. It was September and the autumn rains were on her. By the grace of God, she came down into a valley and heard the grumbling of a hundred thousand sheep. Folded tight in nets, the animals gleamed in the drizzle. Exhausted as she had never been, and wet through, Mme Duclos joined a group of men about their fire. Like shepherds everywhere, they said little but made space for her. She made the men's supper, collected fire-wood and baked some bread in the ashes for morning.

They were shepherds of the district, five men and a boy, who had spent the summer in the mountain pasture, and were taking a thousand head of *merino* ewes to the winter grazing on the banks of the Guadiana. It was a walk of some one hundred fifty leagues, or five hundred miles, through Old Castile by way of Valladolid and Ávila. The tramp would take forty days. In the winter pasture, between All Saints and Christmas Days, the ewes would lamb.

The shepherds spoke among themselves some Romance tongue of the mountains but seemed to understand the straggler's Castilian. Extemporising, Mme Duclos said she was a widow-woman who, left destitute at her husband's death, was seeking to join her daughter at Badajoz. She said she would do the woman's work and ask no wage, only the protection of the shepherds' dogs on the road. The men said nothing. They did not want her or any female. Their mountain honour would not let them turn her away from the fire.

The next morning, once the sun had dried the dew off the grass, they broke camp. Mme Duclos followed behind with the pack animals and the milk-goats, picked up the laggards, gathered green stuff. They followed a sort of high-way or sheep-walk, sometimes marked with stone posts, which the lad called the *cañada*, the sheep grazing at the new autumn grass and always moving, moving. When they came against another flock, Mme Duclos made sure to keep out of sight. In the villages, where men and women stood at their house doors and spat on the earth, Mme Duclos bartered milk and cheese for vinegar and grain.

Mme Duclos saw that there was no place for her, because

there was never any place for a woman on the transhumation. It seemed to her that the shepherds followed laws they did not wholly understand but had been refined over generations: perhaps, even since the disintegration of the Arab Califat and the opening of the southern pastures to the Christian flock-owners five or six centuries before; or perhaps it was the Arab grazing practice turned on its head.

Yet on the periphery of this constitution of grass and wool, Mme Duclos found areas not precisely legislated. There was, for example, no literal injunction against the use of blood sausage on high days in the breakfast food the men called *migas*. The lad or *zagal*, whose name was Pero, had yet to take the shepherd's vow of silence. In company, he spoke to Mme Duclos roughly lest his seniors suspect he missed his mother; but, in the rear of the flock, he chattered away in his mountain Latin. Mme Duclos put that into classical Latin, from Latin into French and from French into Castilian, all in an instant, and they got on mightily. She gave the bell-wethers treats and salved the wounds of the dogs with her vinegar.

The dogs were of great size, called *mastines* by the boy, and brave beyond all imagination. In the mountains, they saw off a she-bear; and in the suburbs of Valladolid, a pack of wolves. At any disturbance, they formed ranks, bellowing like demons, while detachments took off, in silence, to the wings so as to take the enemy in the rear.

The shepherds did not ask her name and she gave none. They called her *la muyer* and addressed her as *oh muyer!*

"Woman! Give the dogs no meat."

Like women since the time of our mother Eve, Mme Duclos made herself pleasant and useful. She wondered if, in the course of this nightmare tramp, law was being made and that henceforth each *rebaño* (as their sub-flock was called) would be attended by a poor, lame crone, running for her life from the Emperor of France.

Mme Duclos thought it just, for the grass-widows in the mountains, that their men should not mix with strange females in the promiscuity of a forty-day tramp. Yet a woman on the tip of her eighth decade? Mme Duclos understood that her education at La Ferté-Joyeuse, first as a kitchen servant and then in study of Latin and its successor-tongues, might have been devised, precisely, for her present style of living. Mme Duclos thought: Were I not so tired at nightfall, or so anxious for Isabelle and young William, I would be happy; and, if I live, I shall forget the pain and fear and remember the tinkling of the bell-wethers, and the smell of wet sheep's wool and dust and dung, and the dogs braver than lions and kinder than kittens and the valleys white with fleeces as with snow.

Yet Mme Duclos felt heavy of heart and that heaviness increased with every night on the road. Something in her trampwoman's existence had broadened her mental range.

At Valladolid, her thoughts gained contour. Mme Duclos said to herself: Mme de Thelles will not forgive me, for I dashed from her head the martyr's crown. While to the world, the sisters had laid down their lives for France and had been reprieved, as France had been reprieved, it was not so to Mme de Thelles. At the Convent of San José, I shall wash the floors and tend the sick in a fog of something like hatred. I am the world and the flesh. They shall shun and, in the end, betray me.

Mme Duclos waited with the animals under the walls of Ávila while the men went into town. They came back at morning, drunk as lords, carrying the lad. Mme Duclos strapped the boy on an ass, as if he were the mortally wounded Cid at the Siege of Valencia. The men bore their oaken heads into New Castile and, then, Extremadura. Thus burdened, they were more than usually taciturn; but Mme Duclos was told by little Pero, once he had found his wits, that if the woman chose to remain with the flock over the winter for the lambing, gelding and culling, she should have her portion of food.

At Cáceres, Mme Duclos felt a breath of wind, soft and cold, scarce strong enough to blow out a candle. She thought that her life was leaving her; and then, with a shock that made her halt, that the soul of someone who held her dear had touched hers as it sped past. Then she knew, for the first time and with certainty, that she had loved the Englishman James Stokes.

XXXIII

The hamlet of Chiselwold in the English county of Kent is one of those places that, for all its rural sweetness, is as cockney as an oyster-seller. Here, in the first years of the nineteenth century, plum- and half-plum-men deteriorated amid honeysuckle. The church of St Ethelbert, with its little square tower, was as trim as a carriage in Hyde-Park.

Sir James Stokes had left on earth two daughters. Both had married noblemen. The matches were made not out of any attachment of the girls to coronets and tumbledown houses, but because dowries and coverture were a special study of that class of men. Augusta, who had married the earl, was not to be troubled by funerary arrangements which fell to Ada, the baronet's lady.

The grief of Ada's life was not her husband, though he was not ideal, but in not acceding to her father's wish that she keep house for him at Paris. Himself sedentary or even immobile, Sir Harbold Harbold wished that his lady also be so. Ada looked about the toy burial-yard in a mood of despair.

The mourners were lean, wiry men and pretty women who had been too much in the sun. Though they seemed acquainted, the one with another, even intimate, each introduced himself by name. Ada had put out a book for them to sign, but none had done so. The King and Queen had sent a wreath, the Prime Minister his carriage. Mr Covington, one of the two members for Harwich, gave the address.

A gentleman with a Scottish name, MacNeill or some-such, stood beside Ada and followed, with modest interest, her gaze.

Ada exclaimed: "I suppose they are all Post Office!"

"I believe they are, madam."

"And after His Majesty's Embassy at Paris!"

"I believe, madam, that your father would have served his country in any capacity, however ordinary."

Ada felt rebuked. She turned at bay.

"May I ask, sir: Who is Mrs Duclos?"

"My sister, ma'am."

Ada, who had thought the person an actress or opera dancer, with little cloven feet and dainty horns peeping out of cataracts of midnight hair, was relieved. Her sons' inheritance was safe.

William had no wish to pry into his sister's connections. Yet Ada, whose picture of her father had been turned upside down, was looking at him in a moral state akin to panic.

"Mme Duclos is a widow-lady, now advanced in years. I believe she corresponded with your father on scientific matters."

Ada was relieved. To think of it, a horrid old *savante*!

"Is Mrs Duclos in England?"

"No, ma'am. I wish above all things that she were."

"Sir James left a letter for your lady sister." Ada looked about the emptying church-yard and the mourners gliding between the yews. In exasperation, she said: "You, sir, at least will join us at the funeral breakfast."

"That would be an honour, madam," William said. His plans for the day he re-arranged like boarding-house furniture preparatory to a visit.

At the breakfast, William was accosted by two young men.

"May I present myself, sir? Godfrey, foreign secretary at the General Post Office," said Tim Tappin. "And also my fellow-labourer in the postal vineyard, Mr Tappin."

Pete Grundon bowed.

William found himself in a corner, Mr Godfrey facing him, Mr Tappin with his back to him.

Mr Godfrey said: *"Veuillez s'il vous plaît sourire, monsieur."*

Kindly smile, sir.

William smiled.

Mr Godfrey continued in French: "On no account is the lady to go to Ávila."

William did not ask why his sister should avoid that holy city. Yet he was, it seemed, in the particular sense of the foreign letter office of the G.P.O, "family", and Mr Godfrey told him.

"Don Patricio Cortés, rector of the Irish College at Salamanca – old Pattie Curtis as was – has made himself confessor to the Irish sisters at the convent. Kindly continue to smile, sir. He is asking questions about the affair of the place du Trône."

"I know nothing of that affair."

"Shall we keep it that way? But you know the English cannon?"

"As a young boy, I discharged it. Twice."

"May I ask the year in which you did so?"

"Seventeen-hundred and sixty."

"Marks of identification?"

"On the first reinforce, 'GR II'. On the base ring: 'W. Bowen fecit 1743'. Bowen's furnace was at Cowden, not far from here."

"Anything else, sir?"

"On the breech ogee, '4-3-24'. That is 556 pounds barrel-weight. On the right trunnion, 'No. 18'.

"*Bougre!*"

Bugger!

"I beg your pardon, sir!"

"He'll trace the piece to Canada and, in the end, to the lady."

"I do not believe so, sir. My mother gave orders to the smith at her country house to obliterate both M. Bowen's signature and the manufacture number."

"May I ask when that was done, sir?"

"In 1760."

William felt the atmosphere lighten.

"A perspicacious lady, if I may be permitted to say so, sir."

On taking his leave, William received from Ada Sir James Stokes' letter. He took it as if it were a rare and fragile creature. He concealed the missive first on his person, then, once returned to London, at Mr Rouquette the banker's in Fleet-Street. William had no doubt it was a declaration of love from a dying man.

It was not.

Sister Augusta had espied the surreptitious transfer. Her lawyer wrote to Mr Rouquette, reminding him that the document was part of the late Sir James Stokes' estate and must be submitted for probate. Mr Rouquette refused. William, whose precarious *émigré* life admitted of no legal entanglements, ordered his financial friend to surrender the letter. (They had become intimate at Mr Rouquette's little musical evenings in Fleet Street, where William supplied the wood-wind.)

In his chambers in Lincoln's Inn, in the presence of a great many persons, Augusta's pettifogger broke the seal. The cover contained a bill of exchange for £5,000 in current money of the country, payable at sight, on the Melekettojjar, or dean of the wholesale merchants' guild, at Tangiers. Enclosed with it was half a gold coin, of ten *dinar* face-value, cut with a jig-saw so as somewhat to resemble a mortice-key. With the agreement of the sisters and William, the lawyer proposed that he should retain the bill, as a contingent liability of the late Sir James Stokes' estate, until such time as Mrs Duclos should present and identify herself. As for the clipped coin, Mr Rouquette asked that he might retain it for a little numismatic museum he had erected at the banking-house. That was conceded.

As William and his friend strolled, arm-in-arm, from Lincoln's Inn to Fleet Street, the banker slipped the whimsical object into his customer's coat-pocket.

Mr Rouquette said: "The matching half of the coin, sir, sits this very moment in the worthy Mohammedan's strong-box. If you can convey this half to the lady, she shall receive every assistance that pious and hospitable nation can furnish."

XXXIV

Mr MacNeill had received no word of his elder son for a dozen years, but had not lost hope of his survival. He believed, rightly as it turned out, that young William was but a nameless contributor to the glory of France and of the greatest Emperor since Charlemagne.

The Peace of Amiens lasted but a year. William and his men, reduced yet further in number, spent the next year at Boulogne, preparing for an invasion of Great Britain. Already master of the hydrography of the rivers of the continent – the Po, the Adige, the Inn, the Danube, the Elbe, the Scheldt,

the Rhine, the Tagus, the Ebro, the Vistula, the Niemen –
William informed himself about the Medway and the
Thames of England.

The annihilation of the French fleet by Admiral Lord
Nelson off Cape Trafalgar in October 1805 put paid to such
ambitions. The project of M. Fleurant, to convey an exped-
itionary force over the intervening water by aerostat and have
them lowered by *parachute*, did not receive the hearing William believed that it deserved.

The pontonniers carried their boats into Germany and, in
the year 1807, built a raft on the left bank of the Niemen at
the town of Tilsit, and moored it in the middle of the river
for a meeting of the emperors of France and Russia. On the
île Lobau by Vienna in 1809, William and his men made a
bridge of one hundred and sixty metres in four sections and
laid it, after midnight, in five minutes. That year, by *ancien-
neté* or length of service, William was made captain of a
new-formed company with a paper or theoretical strength of
one hundred and ten Hollanders.

In all those operations, did William ever see his former
friend?

He did. Having smashed the Tsar's army at Austerlitz in
Bohemia, the Emperor was inclined to be generous. On the
evening of June 24th, 1807, in the town of Tilsit, on the south
or left bank of the River Niemen that separates East Prussia
from the Russian parts of Lithuania, at 9 p.m. by the clock,

Captain William Niellon received a written order to construct a raft "suitable for the reception of Their Majesties the Emperor of France and King of Italy and the Emperor of all the Russias" and tow it out to the hydrographic middle, or *Thalweg*, of the stream by no later than mid-day on the morrow, June 25th, 1807 (which was, by coincidence, the second anniversary of Austerlitz).

William was not in the habit of questioning orders or wondering why the Emperors of such vast territories should want to dally in the middle of a sluggish river. His questions were of a mechanical character: what structures must the raft bear, and how many men, horses, cannon and vehicles? William sought advice from the chief engineer of the Imperial Guard, who said: "Go big, Niellon. As big as you can imagine, then double it."

William had never before made a structure for display.

The Niemen in that flat and marshy country is as placid as an old dog. There was cut timber and to spare in town, and though William would have preferred the poplar wood abundant in the north of Italy (which weighs but twenty-six pounds per cubic metre), fir- and pine-wood were a second-best. While he was at his mathematics, and the Dutchmen were driving up carts of planks from the hangars on the quay, a young Lieutenant of the Guard brought him a sketch and elevations for three pavilions that would not have shamed the Field of the Cloth of Gold.

William said: "You fellows build them. If we do so, Their Imperial Majesties will be under mud and thatch."

In the mid-summer twilight, they barely needed torches. The Immortals jeered from the bank and, from the water, the Dutchmen sent up profanities. By eleven in the morning, the pavilions were in place with their garlands and festoons; and, twenty minutes later the contraption, held by six anchors, swam precisely in mid-river.

The armies, drawn up on both banks in full-dress, were a sight to behold: less so, the raft-builders, squeezed into uniforms, faces spattered with mud, shakos awry. At 1 p.m., a flotilla of gay vessels detached itself from the opposite or right bank with, in the bow of the lead barge, a handsome young man William took to be the Tsar. William was looking at the anchor cables, to be sure they were taut, and at the break of the stream on the bow of the raft.

From the lee of the chief pavilion, a figure appeared, bareheaded, not tall, somewhat filled out at the waist and chest, right hand extended in greeting, and on his face the look of a benevolent uncle about to shower a promising nephew in favour. Even at a distance of one hundred yards and twenty-two years, William saw the boy in the Emperor of the World.

He did not remark the Tsar's attendants, least of all a tall officer of His Tsarian Majesty's Horse Guard with a shock of yellow hair.

Austerlitz was the first battle in which the Guard were

engaged. From his station on a ridge, Captain Count Bielke could see the right wing bend like a bow. The battle, he thought, is lost before it has started. At that moment, a mortar-shell burst on the sod to his right, killing the brigade commander and covering our friend in bloody guts.

Raising his sabre, with a shout of "With Bielke!", he spurred his mount downhill.

"With Bielke! With Bielke!" came the roar at his back.

The French infantry formed square, but their volley, when it came, was half-a-second too late. Dead men and wounded horses crashed into the ranks and, through the breaches, the Cavalier Guard rode through. Count Bielke saw before him the French standard, abandoned where it stood in the heart of the square. Running towards it was a drummer-boy, his boots too big for him, tunic flapping, shako awry.

Count Bielke reined in, and pulled the eagle from the ground. The lad caught the butt end.

Count Bielke said: "I do not wish to kill you, brave Frenchman."

"But you must, sir."

Count Bielke let go. The release of force sent the lad sprawling on his back. Count Bielke swung low in the saddle and retrieved the eagle.

"Live well, *mon brave français*," he said. Then, with a cry of "With Bielke!", Count Bielke rode out of the shattered square. Looking back, he saw the lad had picked up a musket, and was squinting down the jumping barrel at him. The ball passed over his head.

"With Bielke!"

In a shower of blood and water, they reached the headquarters' troop. On the Emperor's face was a look that said: Nobody informed me that battles could be lost as well as won. Handing the French eagle to a staff officer, Count Bielke wheeled the troop about and then, as if they had been on parade at the Winter Palace in Peter, walked them backwards. Taking the advice, the Tsar, Archduke Constantine and all the fools who had sought the fight withdrew from the battlefield.

That day, the Imperial Russian army captured a French eagle, and lost forty-three of their own.

In Saint Petersburg, all thought that Count Bielke was now untameable. No man, it was said, and in especial no husband, would be safe from him. Nothing of that character occurred. I do not say that Count Bielke had become a General Ireton who, when slapped by a subordinate, offered the other cheek. Yet if some puffed-up Balt sought a quarrel with the famous Count Bielke, that officer might propose a drinking-bout, or a swim across the frozen Fontanka, or a test of strength. Only if those trials were rejected would our friend wound the bold fellow.

Count Bielke was haunted by the drummer-boy at Austerlitz. It was not that he had come upon someone braver than himself: nothing so foolish or commonplace. It was as if he had been given a glimpse of something beyond the sensuous world and indescribable in the speech of that world. Count Bielke spoke of the episode to nobody, man or woman.

Except one.

He told the story with his bare back turned.

In the flicker of the night-light, Isabelle saw on her husband's back a scar from left shoulder to right hip. She resisted an urge to trace the scar with her fingers.

From the edge of sleep, Isabelle said: "He is the privilege of your life, Count Bielke. Do not squander him."

Count Bielke turned and looked down at his sleeping wife. He thought to say: You are the privilege of my life. He came to it, but it was a step too far.

PART 4

Over the River

XXXV

Captain William Niellon walked across the court of the Petrowskoïe Palace. It was the evening of September 15th, 1812.

Rising in the night sky to the south and east was the most beautiful sight that had ever come before his eyes, even in dreams. His people made space for him.

Before him was a pyramid of coppery smoke, and beneath it sheaves of fire waving like ripe barley in a gale. There was a whistling, and the snap and crack of explosions whether from powder in the magazines on the river wharves, or oil and spirits in the shops. The wind at his back all but knocked William to his knees.

The city of Moscow was on fire.

William had seen great cities, had seen Paris, Cairo, Vienna, Berlin, Madrid and Warsaw. He had, not a month before, seen the city of Smolensk burn. Nothing approached the sight of Moscow fired by its own people.

"Are you coming to the Fair, Captain? We call it Moscow Fair!"

Sergeant Jeff was one of those sub-officers that are indispensable to a military force. Only such men know what the common soldiers will tolerate by way of hardship, or what the commissioned officers will permit by way of licence. Subordination is not a Dutch virtue. Jeff marched on beer, and much of his leisure was given to finding hops.

William believed that, though he was a murderer, he was not yet a thief. He thought: It is the Emperor's bad example, in stripping every town of its treasures and antiquities and carting them to Paris. Had M. Buonaparte the engineers when we were in Egypt, he would have dug out the Sphinx.

"No. Roll-call at 10 p.m."

"In your dreams, Willem."

Marietje, the company *vivandière* or seller of provisions, was a lady past her first youth, and had not yet decided whether she was principally a siren or at top a mother, being sometimes the one, and sometimes the other, and sometimes both at once. Why she had abandoned Purmerend, on the rich polder, was a secret. She seemed to William to have loved more than she had been loved.

"The captain shall stay with me," she said, putting William's arm about her waist.

That night at roll-call, William missed a dozen men. They straggled in at dawn, their tunics scorched, their faces black, dragging their booty and prisoners. They spoke of palaces on fire, streets littered with fine furniture and lustres, incendiarists lined up by the Poles against the flames and shot down.

Mother Marietje had seized two cart-loads of white cabbages and was making choucroute, which the Dutch call *zuurkool*, on the bare ground for the winter. The stragglers received knives, salt and pitch-forks under her orders, a cruel and unusual punishment for scalded hands and sore heads. As for William, he passed the day directing the farriers at the forge, sharp-shoeing the horses. The weather was glorious, and William worked at the bellows in his shirt, but he knew that at some point that autumn the horses would need to go over ice.

On the second night of fire, the men had a fright. They had captured four Russian men with torches, whom they took to be fire-starters, and put them in the shafts of the wagon of spoils. As they passed the Kremlin castle between two walls of flame, the iron roof of a nobleman's palace detached itself, and, spitting gobbets of molten metal, fell into the street, incinerating cart, booty and Russians. Beset on all sides by the fire, the men barely managed to reach the river and wait out the flames.

Next morning, Jeff and the under-officers took stock. They had said at Dantzig that they would be rich, and they were. From the great emporium of the East, they had gathered up two hundred bottles of Jamaica rum, the same of

Champagne, confit fruits, sugar loaves for making punch, a barrel of suet, three dozen hams, much salted fish, Cachemire shawls, silks, icons, silver crosses and mousselines. Prize of all was a magnificent wine-cooler of colossal size, the silver chased with designs of nymphs and satyrs up to every sort of open-air frolic, which was to serve on high days as company punch-bowl. William had noted before that the Dutch men had a great notion of comfort. They were looking forward to a cosy winter in Moscow.

The men had engaged a tailor and a laundress, whom they had, at great risk, brought out of the fire.

Since the army had come into Russia without winter clothes, the tailor was set to making neck-warmers from a bolt of billiard-table cloth. The lady appeared to William quite handsome for a *blanchisseuse* but, whatever her other duties, Mlle Nadia was good with linen; and the presence of women, whatever their moral character, always improves the appearance and deportment of men.

Sometimes, even a good officer must turn a blind eye.

For the moment, the weather was delicious.

XXXVI

They had set off in April from Dantzig on the Baltic in high spirits: eight companies of bridge-men, one hundred and twenty boats with their carriages, one hundred vehicles loaded with charcoal, cut timber and lifting-gear, eight mobile forges and two thousand horses. Some said they would beat Russia, as they had done at Austerlitz and Friedland, then carry them along as allies to Bengal or even China. They would return to Holland rich and wise.

On June 23rd, commencing in the twilight at 11 p.m., they built in three and three-quarters hours over the Niemen river above Kowno three pontoon bridges, each of thirty-three boats and one hundred toises in length.

In his thirty years of soldiering, William had trained himself to have no thoughts above his rank, first as a sub-lieutenant, then sergeant, lieutenant and captain. He had shut off parts of his mind rather as a country gentleman, unsuccessful in his rural operations, or ruined by daughters, shuts off the side-wings of his house.

Yet, on the river bank, politics found him.

France had not been so strong or extensive since Charlemagne, and had never been so rich. She had remade Germany, Poland and Italy; had Spain and Austria at heel; was again on good terms with the Sublime Porte at Constantinople. Yet even as the Emperor humbled the old powers, turned the proud republics of Holland and Switzerland into vassals, and bought off the Americans with the gift of Louisiana, so new powers had risen to fill the vacated spaces: Great Britain, safe behind her wooden walls, and Russia in all her vastness. All

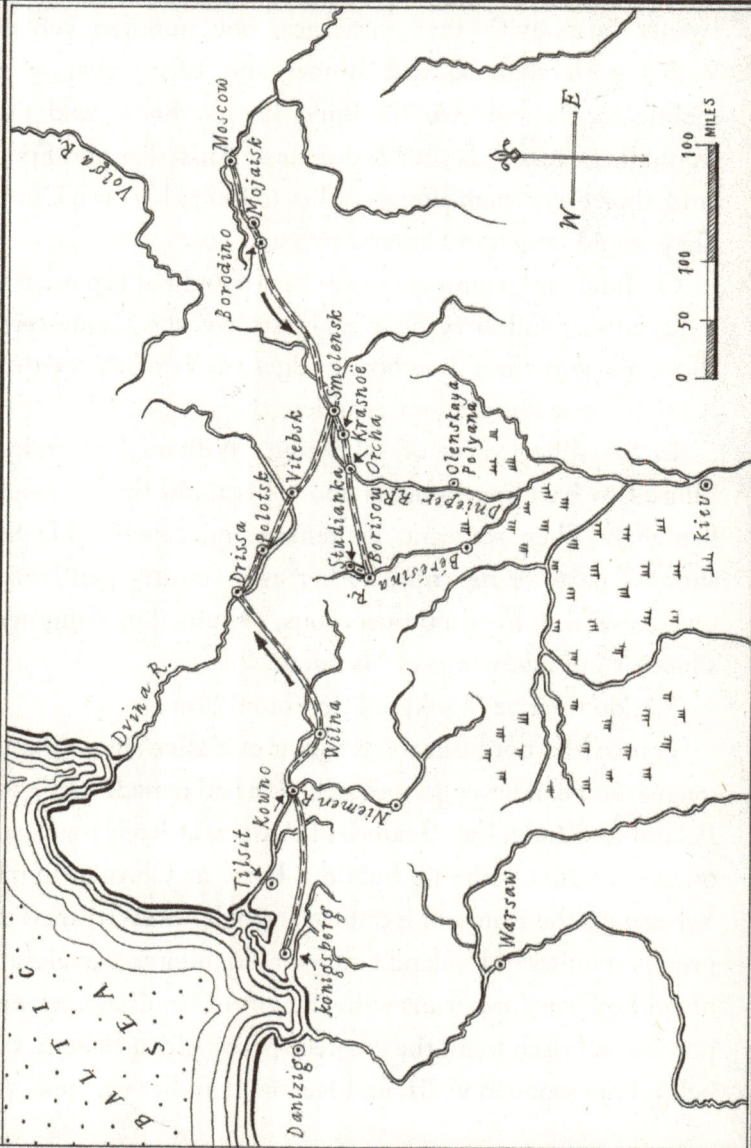

CAPTAIN NIELLON in RUSSIA, 1812

France, from the Emperor down, was on a treadmill of victory.

Russia had been growing like a prize stall-beast for more than a hundred years. She had dealt with her ancient enemies, the Kings of Sweden and the Ottoman Sultans. Under the Tsaritsa Catherine, she had overrun eastern Ukraine and taken Kiev, the Crimea and the shores of the Black Sea, broken through the Caucasus, and driven the Persians out of Georgia. With the dismemberment of Poland, she had inherited a great number of Jews which she sought to keep out of old Russia. Further east, she cast her shadow over the Khanates and the English in distant Calcutta. She now wished to give law to Poland and the German states and had massed an army on the far or right bank of the Niemen. She must expunge the shame of Austerlitz from the slate.

The *guerrilla* in Spain was no longer a little war. The English had found, to their surprise and satisfaction, that one may fight on land as well as water and in Lord Wellington, commander in Portugal and Spain, they had an officer to show them how terrestrial war is conducted.

By its example, France had shown what a nation could be. The feeling of national purpose that had given France its victory at Valmy had taken hold in Spain and the German states and principalities, and was stirring in the Italian peninsula and Sicily. It was not as William had found in Egypt and Syria, where men wanted nothing from France because their customs and religion gave them all that they required. Rather, whatever benefits French rule had brought to the nations in Europe, they were annulled by the Frenchness of France.

Those races cared nothing for a universal monarchy, a single code of laws and court of appeal, a common currency, rational weights and measures, a nobility of merit: in all, a unified Europe with its capital at Paris in which all their treasures would be displayed to their best advantage. They preferred to govern themselves badly than be well governed by France.

As William watched the Grande Armée cross the three bridges into Russia in blazing sunshine, the regiments in full dress and perfect order behind their bands and then the hordes of camp-followers, a half-million combatants and non-combatants, devouring everything in their passage, an oracle from the school-room at La Brienne whispered in Greek in his ear: If you take an army against the Persians, you shall destroy a great empire. Another thought was that, if they succeeded, which William thought unlikely, he might be of some use to Isabelle at Deer's Glade, and to her husband.

The going was hard. It was as hot as ever Spain, the country stripped of food and forage by the retreating Russians, the road-sides foul with shit and dead horses. They drove in a fog of dust. Flies and gnats tormented them. Lice infested their clothes. Men started to fall down, the youngest first: the drummer-boys and both lieutenants, the one to pleurisy, the other to exhaustion. In the crush of the column, William was happy to make twenty miles in a day. Cosaques on bony horses hovered just out of shot, or Bachkir horsemen from the Urals loosed off storms of arrows. The men laughed and jeered at those antique weapons until Joost was spitted through the throat.

In the night of July 2nd, almost in sight of Wilna, a storm burst and engulfed them in freezing rain. The men found shelter under the wagons, but the horses suffered agonies, and fully a quarter died either that night or toiling through the mud in the succeeding days. William commandeered oxen to replace them. They passed new-built redoubts and fortifications, as if the Russians had intended to give battle but thought better of it.

They lashed together rafts to take the army over the Dvina at Drissa, and the Dnieper at Orcha, where they left half the boats to spare their horses to draw the heavy guns. They laid bridges over the Dnieper at Smolensk, with the city in flames about them, the streets strewn with burned corpses.

The army was marching on a broad front. The companies were separated, and the men were constantly at work bridging ravines and torrents with whatever timber lay to hand. William's company, which had started under-strength at Dantzig, was now down to its captain and forty-five under-officers and men. William blessed that they were in the vanguard and did not see what was behind them.

Finally, on September 7th, at a place called Borodino, the Russian armies made a stand. The fight was hard, and even at the rear the bridging-train came under well-directed cannon-fire, but by evening the Russians withdrew, leaving the Emperor in command of the day and the battlefield. It did not feel like victory.

XXXVII

At the Petrowskoïe, William allowed the men a week of absolute licence. On the last night, they held a carnival ball, the men dressed as boyars, mandarins, Jews from beyond the Pale and who knows what and the ladies as noblewomen of the Old Régime of France.

The next morning, October 13th, William did his round of the corpses.

He said: "Drink up, Sergeant. We shall soon be on the move."

"Bollocks, Willem. The Russians are licked. The Emperor has opened the theatres and churches."

"We are going home."

"Tits! Retreat is impossible in this country. And it is too late in the year to march on Peter."

"There is nothing here to sustain an army, even one like ours reduced by two-thirds. The city is cleaned out. The peasants are burning their grain rather than let us have it. There is no fodder for the horses."

"Shit," said Sergeant Jeff.

"Inform the men."

"You fucking do it. You got us here, Willem. You get us back again."

"I shall. And I shall."

"Two weeks was enough to clear out this place. Why did the Emperor have to wait for winter? He's no better than a fucking recruit."

That afternoon, William received orders to abandon the pontoons and wagons.

He obeyed, but not to the letter. The boats he burned. Amid the smoke, in the stable wing of the palace, he hid the field forge, a cart of charcoal and another of tools, their teams and Marietje.

He said: "We must keep to the head of the column, where there will still be shelter and even post-houses and villages with something in them."

As they prepared to move out, they were overrun by swarms of traders, who had come from town to exchange food and brandy for the men's valuables.

Among the milling pedlars, William saw a young man, a head taller than the others, strong and well-shaped.

William said: "You, sir! Do you speak German?"

"*Jidisch.*"

Jewish.

"*Kum mit undz. Es vet zeyn handl.*"

Come with us. There will be commerce, and to spare.

The traders, disturbed in their bartering, turned on the handsome lad.

"*Ish ken nisht geyn tsu fus.*"

I cannot march.

"You shall ride in the supply wagon."

The offer of transportation, and for a mere lad, brought uproar among his seniors.

Somebody shouted in Jewish: "Tsar will kill them all on the road, and you, too, Avraam Iankelovitch."

Now, all the merchants wished to be of the party, to the extent that the men had to push them back with their rifle-stocks.

Mother Marietje was outraged at the invasion of her sanctum, but seeing the ringlets tumbling from beneath the youth's broad hat, a pair coal-black eyes and the same of ruby lips, the lady softened. Of all the Christian nations of Europe, the Dutch are, unless that be the Scots, the least hostile to the Jewish nation.

Mother Marietje said: "Come up by me, laddie, and we'll be snug."

Sergeant Jeff had his hands on his hips.

"What are you doing, Willem?"

William took the sub-officer apart. He said: "Do you remember those Jew villages we passed through before Smolensk?"

Jeff nodded.

"The lad will know where we may find barley and hops."

Jeff said: "You're an arsehole, Willem, but you're a good officer."

William feared that the men would take with them their Russian mistresses. As far as he could tell, the ladies preferred to stay in a city burned to its foundations and over-run by brigands. The men appeared relieved, but not William. The dread that had come on him at the Niemen gnawed at his belly.

XXXVIII

On October 19th, 1812, the bridge train received its marching orders. Before they broke out, William had the notion that he should address the men. Not given to oratory, he summoned every ounce of eloquence.

"You glories of Holland, kings of the ditches, emperors of mud! If you leave me for a moment, you are fucked. I say again, if you do not follow me, you are fucked. If you fall out of the company, you are fucked. If you stop to help a comrade, you are fucked. If you take up a pretty mother and her child, you are fucked. If you go out to forage, you are fucked. If you drop your weapon, you are fucked. If you loose your musket at a Cosaque, you are fucked. If you are taken prisoner, you are fucked."

"Fuck you, Captain."

"Fuck off, Willem."

"Good. We understand one another."

They set off, the men crooked by the weight of treasure in their knapsacks, their cross-belts clanking with silver spoons and ladles, their game sacks overflowing with icons, about their necks bear-skins and sables. They were fed and rested. Out of delicacy of feeling, they bivouacked the first night a little apart from Mother Marietje's wagon.

At first, they moved southwards but, coming on the chief Russian forces, commanded by Marshal Koutousoff, after a sharp engagement they wheeled right and found themselves once again amid the devastation of the Smolensk road. Near Mojaisk, the night of October 27th–28th brought the first frost. The next morning, they came down into a plain which seemed, to William's first impression, pastured by flocks of fat sheep. Then William saw that they were not sheep but, bloated and stripped of all covering, the bodies of the dead of the Battle of the Moskva at Borodino. Before the V-shaped *flèches* and redoubts the Russians had erected were drifts of spent musket balls and canister-shot like fresh hail. From the convent nearby, they took up a dozen men wounded in the battle, but the jolting of the wagons caused the poor men agonies and their cries dispirited the men. None of the wounded survived the day.

The only enemy they saw were Cosaques on their lean ponies, at a distance, watching the column like jackals following an injured animal. William learned the delight of drinking water from a pond free of corpses and the taste of frozen munition bread. At bivouac, they ate up everything they had brought from Moscow.

The next night but one, they had their first snow. William began to see by the road discarded booty. M. Avraam would skip down from the box of the wagon, pick up a folio, leaf through it, put it down; examine a candelabrum, weigh it in his hands, set it down upright; then scoop something small from a puddle and bury it in the folds of his caftane. The horses were so weak that they had to harness three pairs to the wagons. He saw artillery pieces dragged forward foot-by-foot by twelve suffering hacks. William drove the wagons on, shouting at the top of his voice: "Bridging-train to the front! Bridging-train to the front!" That was successful once, but not again.

In the night of the new moon, November 4th–5th, the thermometer dropped to −12 degrees Réaumur. It was from that night that William marked the disintegration of the Grande Armée. Men ceased to share food. They abandoned the dead and wounded in their bivouacs. Lost men stumbled through the snowflakes crying "First Corps!" or "Imperial Guard!"

Those horses not sharp-shod could not move on the ice. They were slaughtered where they stood and the wagons abandoned. Mobs of stragglers, of every nation under heaven, encumbered the crossings, stealing anything they could find or begging for food, while women sat sprawled in heaps, holding up their infants and begging the company to take them. The sight of the broken men instilled the men with pity, but also with fear; for they knew, even if William had not told them, that only if they kept order might they save their lives. The stragglers might have been lepers.

Often William had to leave the beaten road, and cross fields by the light of burning farms, the horses up to their bellies in the snow. At Dorogobouj, on November 6th, a thick fog came down. William's lips stuck together and he had no fat to keep them apart. In a corner of a barn, they found a heap of frozen cattle-roots which the Dutchmen called *kool-raap*. The men fell on them as if they had been Chambrette pears. Before they could break their teeth, Mother Marietje interposed, set the men to cleaning the roots and lighting the fire; herself bled one of the horses at the throat; applied some sprouted oats; and made a porridge. On the night of the 8th, the thermometer dropped to −28 degrees Réaumur and the company lost six men, frozen stiff in their places.

They were tormented by lice. Sometimes, a man would spring up from the fire and, with a terrible howling, roll himself in a drift of snow.

"Quit complaining," said William. "The Emperor has lice. Does he complain?"

And then: "M. Avraam, shall we make sleds for the wagons?"

The youth shook his head. He said: "There will be a thaw."

There was, and they plodded on in mud as thick and foul as a peasant's pig-sty in winter.

By trial and error, William had found a system. The days were shortening, and he called halt at early afternoon at any place where there were abandoned coaches or a birch copse to provide fuel. Doors with intricate liveries, silk cushions, wheels and harness went up in flames. Their own wagons William had chained in a line east to west, and the horses unhitched, unbitted and picketed in the lee of the north wind. They made cabins of dry boughs. Mother Marietje cooked horse-meat bouillon with a handful of flour or rice thrown in it. M. Avraam, who had been bred up as a cobbler, repaired the men's boots with birch-bark and cat-gut. The men slept or tended the fire, or stood guard over the horses and wagons, in relays of a quarter-hour. William slept standing. Every hour, they walked the horses so they should not freeze.

Broken men crowded the edge of the fire-light, but

received nothing without first displaying their wares to M. Avraam.

They set out before dawn so as to keep to the head of the column.

XXXIX

On the 10th, they skeltered down wooded ravines into what had been the city of Smolensk. In three weeks' marching, they had covered scarcely three hundred versts or two hundred miles. The men were elated that they would at last find supply and, above all things, bread. What they received was a handful of barley flour, some oatmeal and an ounce of biscuit. Together with 2nd Company, they built two trestles over the Dnieper between the east and west of town and were, perhaps, glad to forget their misery in doing something of their own will.

It was here that Avraam Iankelovitch proved his worth. The streets were deep in snow or sprawled with blackened corpses from the fire, and infested with stragglers, some still with their arms. The Guard had established a sort of bazar in what had been the main place in town, but Avraam led a party of eight men into the back lanes, where they descended flights of steps to snowed-in doors where he listened for an age before gesturing the men to break the doors down. They came back under two sacks of sprouted grain, some pressed tobacco and, best of all, a barrel of salt.

It was not simply that salt is a more savoury seasoning for horse-flesh than cartridge-powder. The salt permitted Marietje to keep the horse-meat from freezing in the wine-cooler, which had been converted into a *saloir* or brine-crock, much to its detriment. In recognition of her new married condition, she had sewn a canvas slip for the vessel so as to conceal the Sardanapalian antics.

They brought the wagons into a ruined church, and soon had a fire going. Marietje made cubes of bouillon of cat- and dog-meat, salt and tallow candles for fat.

The men seemed affected by the place. William could find no organ (for such are not employed in the Eastern church) but he did find a species of flute or pipe, and he picked out Bach's setting of *Nun danket alles Gott* and, after a time, the men joined in singing the hymn. The music, coming out in gusts over the snow-bound streets, started to draw in stragglers and William called a halt. That night, his thermometer read −19 degrees Réaumur.

XL

Without waiting for orders, William set off on the 12th with the vanguard. It had warmed to two or three degrees of the thermometer. The thaw saturated the men's boots. They passed through tumble-down Jewish villages, where there was no food or forage. Indeed, M. Avraam sometimes gave them of their own feeble stock. He must have received intelligence in return, for at times he led the men off the road and into thick fir-woods to avoid strong bands of stragglers or partisans.

On November 18th, at mid-night, two men stumbled into the post-house yard where William had set up bivouac. Once they were unfrozen, they told their tale. They were survivors of 2nd Company, who were attached to the rearguard under Marshal Ney. They had been late starting from Smolensk, were separated from the division before them, and came under attack from four sides. The Marshal was killed or taken. Likewise, the whole of their company.

The report plunged the men into gloom. If Ney was dead, the bravest man of the age and Prince of the Moskva, what hope was there for the remnant of the army! They plodded on through hard frosts, interspersed with floods from the thaw, the north wind always on their right, mouths full of snow to quench their incessant thirst. Many of the horses were so weak that they collapsed in the traces.

The next morning, as they picked their way through the drifts, William saw that one of the wagons was missing. Climbing a rise, he saw that the *vivandière*'s wagon had, for whatever reason, lagged behind. He could just make out, through the mist, Avraam coaxing the team forward.

From a knot of Cosaques to his left, two detached themselves and plunged down amid the drifts. William understood, with a start, that the Russians were quite as hungry as they were. From under his Shabat fur-hat, Avraam observed the riders with interest.

Cosaque horsemen carry no musket, but rather a long wooden pike with an iron point one or two feet long, and any number of wicked knives in their belts. Sergeant Jeff shouldered his carbine, and loosed a shot into the fog. The whole company was struggling back but, as in a nightmare, coming no nearer.

"Shoot, for God's sake, Avraam!"

M. Avraam reached into his bag of treasures. At last, he found what appeared to be a pistol.

"Shoot, for the love of God, Avraam!"

For a while, the youth examined the firing pan. The leading Cosaque had his pike couched against his saddle. His pony was flying over the crust of snow.

He was not ten feet away when Avraam raised his pistol, looked down the barrel, and shot him in the face. The pony crashed into the wagon and lay, thrashing, in the snow.

The second man was coming. It was a tactic of the Cosaques to draw a shot and then close in before the musket could be recharged. The man spurred on.

The flap of the wagon opened. A woman's bare arm emerged through the vent, and in it an antique duelling piece with its match lit. The morning light flashed off its pearl-and-silver hand-piece. Avraam took it and brushed the handle with his sleeve. Seeing the weapon, the Cosaque reined in, made to turn about, but his horse slipped and came down on its rump and, as he struggled in the saddle, Avraam shot him in the chest.

"M. Avraam, you are Gideon and Joshua in one!"

Marietje, in chemise and shawl, without cap, hair loose, appeared from under the canvas. She sparkled at the praise for her lover. Avraam sprang down, rifled the Cosaques' saddle-bags, found something and put it back, then handed Sergeant Jeff a sheet of pressed tobacco. The men cut the throats of the ponies, slit the bellies, pulled out heart and liver, and carried the nourishment to the saloir.

That evening, in the blazing light from the fire, William saw Marietje combing M. Avraam's hair, as if the lad were a Spartiate at Thermopylae.

XLI

On November 19th, the thirty men of the company reached Orcha. There, to their unspeakable joy, they found 7th and 11th Companies, who had come down with the left wing of the army from Vitebsk and Polotsk. The two companies had been on short commons, but were like Household

Guardsmen in comparison with the flapping scarecrows who had walked to Moscow and back. The men embraced one another like family.

Better still, they had brought down sixty-three pontoon boats built at Dantzig for the Niemen crossing, with some five hundred draught-horses, rested and in adequate fettle. There was a little flour and eau-de-vie and, in one of those quirks of military supply, an abundance of fresh clothing. William had the men strip off their infected rags and burn them. As if that were not comfort enough, they heard on the morrow that Ney had broken through the Russian encirclement and, by a feat of endurance extraordinary even for his corps, swum across the Dnieper upstream from Smolensk and, by a wide bow, come down to Orcha.

The relief was but for a day. Summoned to a conference with their commander, General Eblé, in a hut with a smokey fire, the officers were told that the pontoons were to be burned and the fresh horses transferred to the artillery park to draw the cannon and caissons.

All but blinded by smoke, William spoke up. He said: "It would have been better to bury sixty artillery pieces, or otherwise render them unusable, and to preserve the teams for the pontoons. How otherwise shall the army cross the Bérésina? We will have to pray the bridge at Borisow still stands."

"Are you questioning His Majesty's order, Captain Niellon?"

"No, my general," William said. "I know that you shall have done so."

Eblé scowled and then coughed fit to shake to pieces.

Jean-Baptiste Eblé looked older than his fifty-odd years. Born in a village in Lorraine, the son of a sergeant in the Auxonne regiment of artillery, at the age of nine the lad had followed his father into that service. After labouring unseen for twenty-four years, at the outbreak of war in 1792, Eblé was second battery captain.

In a succession of sieges in the Low Countries, Eblé showed his vigour and his imagination. The next year, in the space of two months, he was battalion commander, brigadier and then general commanding the whole artillery of the Army of the North. Men said he was the emblem of what war and revolution could make of an active officer whatever his birth and manners: what the Emperor called *la carrière ouverte aux talents*, the career open to talent. Yet M. Eblé's barony, braid and Freemason's apron had not displaced but was laid over his long subalternity. General Eblé could out-swear the most profane trooper.

Appointed to command the bridging-train, he made no secret of his ignorance of pontoons, rafts and rivers. At Dantzig, he squeezed his staff officers till they squeaked. He spent much time with the company captains and sub-officers, and William as much as any. On the Nogat, to the east of the port-city, General Eblé said to our friend: "You have served your time in lashing boats, Niellon. You shall be my aide-de-camp."

William replied: "With respect, my general, I prefer to stay with my Dutchmen."

"As you please," said General Eblé.

Now, eyes weeping from the smoke, the general said: "You gentlemen decide what you shall take."

Out in the air, William broke the news to the men.

There was uproar.

"Who cares if the Russians take the guns as trophies and place them in front of the Tsar's palace in Peter. We have the fucking Bérésina to cross."

"There will be time enough and place enough for such debates, but it is not here or now. Do you understand, men?"

"Just a recruit!"

"Silence! You will take with you your weapons, sixty cartridges, hammer, axe, two pounds of nails, four pairs of cramp-irons. Captain Benthien and 11th Company will bring a single forge and its fuel. Understood?"

From above the heads of the men, William could see M. Avraam beckoning from the door of the cart-shed.

"Understood?"

"Fuck you."

"Dismissed."

*

In the gloom of the shed, Avraam came so close to William that they touched.

"*Ish vel da bleyben.*"

I am staying here.

William nodded. He said: "Have you told Mother Marietje?"

The lad tutted at William as if to say: What sort of man do you think me to be?

William nodded.

"Don't tell the soldiers. They will kill me for my stock-in-trade."

"They shall not. You are their brother-in-arms."

Avraam held out something in his mittens, but kept his fingers clasped.

William said: "How do we go over the river?"

"Borisow. Wood bridge."

"If it has been demolished?"

The boy looked from side to side.

"Upstream, ten verst, at Studianka. There is a ford. Below the hamlet of Wesselowo."

Avraam opened his hands. Resting in his palms was a sphere of amber, the size of a six-pound round shot.

William closed the lad's fingers over it, turned and walked into the falling snow.

Marietje was in her wagon.

"Courage, mother."

"Go away, captain."

William sat down on the tail-board. He waited, and waited.

Marietje said: "I shall not love again."

"Nonsense, mother! You shall love again and be happy. And on Sunday, you will walk with your fiancé in sunshine above the polder."

"Do you promise, captain?"

"I promise."

XLII

They set off on November 21st, preceded as ever by swarms of stragglers. The road was deep in mud from the thaw, and the bitter wind from the north cut at them, but they were now a military force: the better part of four hundred men, with their arms and tools, in seven broken companies. All around them were marshals, generals, ladies, colonels, cavalrymen, fantassins of every nation, all mixed up hoggledy-piggledy, with every distinction of rank and order abolished. They were, everyone from the Emperor downwards, just pairs of feet.

They reached Borisow in the early afternoon of November 25th.

It was as William had feared. The Russians had taken the town. They had been cleared out two days before by General

Oudinot of II Corps, but after crossing over the Bérésina, the Russians had burned the pile bridge. William sought out General Eblé and gave him M. Avraam's intelligence.

General Oudinot had set up his head-quarters a mile outside town, in a country house belonging to some gentleman or *Pan* with French or Polish sympathies. It had been ransacked, the furniture stacked up and burned in the middle of the tall rooms, the windows smashed, piles of excrement in every corner. Against the walls, staff officers were swaddled in every species of cape, fur and animal skin. General Oudinot, who had been with the left wing at Vitebsk, alone maintained some military bearing.

William said his piece.

General Oudinot, who seemed determined to preserve some of the *élan* of the Grande Armée, burst out laughing.

"You brought a Jew pedlar from Moscow? Amusing."

"For precisely such an emergency, sir."

An officer said: "The Jews here are all for Russia. How do you know, Captain Niellon, that the tinker is not in Russian pay?"

"Avraam Iankelovitch fought like a lion in our company at Krasnoë, sir." Then, much to his surprise, William added: "I believe he may have had hopes of our *vivandière*."

Such a morsel of urbanity, speared and dragged up from long-abandoned depths of William's nature, worked a wonder.

General Oudinot said: "Fetch the amorous youth to me!"

"M. Avraam remained at Orcha, sir."

While William's statement was true, "remained" is one of many military euphemisms for "lost his life".

General Oudinot turned to one of the officers.

"You have my apology, General Corbineau."

From the pit of his furs, a cavalryman spoke. "There is no call for apology, sir. I am delighted that this enterprising engineer-officer has brought corroboration from an unrelated source."

General Corbineau turned to William and said, with wonderful candour: "A detachment of my Polish lancers on the right bank came on a moudzhik who showed them the ford opposite . . ."

He struggled with the name.

"Studianka."

"Thank you. Studianka."

"Excellent, gentlemen. I shall attempt to persuade His Imperial Majesty. Are you mounted, Captain Niellon?"

"No, sir."

"We can probably mount you."

XLIII

It was twilight by the time they came to the ford. The river was not wide, just thirty metres, and did not look at all deep, but the near bank was so marshy in the thaw that William reckoned that the bridges would need to be twice that in length. Above the marsh on their side was a cluster of abandoned wooden cottages. Immense blocks of ice, broken by the thaw, bumped and jostled as they swam downstream. The far bank was steep and a mass of mud. At the top, a picket of Russians were making their supper.

"Can you swim, Benthien?"

"No. Can you, Niellon?"

"Yes. Kindly light a fire. Disperse those fellows on the far bank with a shot or two, but without ostentation. Have one of the men cut me a ten-foot staff, marked at one-foot intervals. And chase the sappers off the houses! We shall need the timber."

William undressed and shook off his boots. The water was scarcely colder than the ambient air. The flow was steady, without strong eddies, but at times he had to swim to evade the blocks of ice. At mid-stream, the depth was but six feet, but only to the surface of the muddy bottom. As he prodded the mud, a howitzer round came in and sent the Russian picket scuttling up the bank, leaving their fire and supper.

William was cramped in both legs, calf and thigh. He yet had some life in his arms, and swam back to the eastern side. Benthien hauled him up from the marsh, put a cape on him and held him upright before the fire.

William looked up. Before him in the fire-light were six

or seven horsemen, with their reins loose, waiting for him to speak. One, easily distinguished by his fur hat and heron feather, was the King of Naples. Beside him were the Prince of Neuchâtel, the Duke of Reggio and Marshal Ney, Prince of Moscow. Also, on foot and, as ever, with his hat in his hand, dear General Eblé. Amid so many kings, princes and famous warriors, William wondered if he were not on the plain of Troy.

William tried to speak but could not. The King of Naples reached into his breast, pulled out something, tossed it to Benthien, who caught it. It was a flask. Benthien poured the brandy into William's mouth. The diamonds on the neck of the flask lacerated William's lips.

"Keep it," said the King.

William said: "We have not the time to drive in piles, nor is there timber enough for rafts. We must build a trestle-bridge."

"If this damn'd country has anything, it has woods."

"The horses do not have the strength to haul timber from the woods. Those houses will supply the material. Two bridges, one hundred toises apart. Fifty-four toises in length. Twenty-three trestles of between three and eight feet in height, set at distances of fourteen feet.

"To protect my men, I request that order be given to stage a feint, either at Borisow or at the place where Charles of Sweden crossed, years ago, I do not know its name but the

Russians do." William did know. For a captain of pontonniers, he had talked enough.

Having trained himself, over more than twenty-five years,
to expunge any trace of his familiar upbringing, and to be
precise, technical, stolid and mechanical, William was yet
affected by the heroic character of the scene. He was standing, all but naked, amid paladins, gathered from humble
places all over France by the whirlwind of Buonaparte's
genius. Yet their glories and victories, their vigour, their
superhuman bravery, their charges and battles, their king-
doms, principalities, millions, mistresses; indeed, the whole
history of Europe and near Asia would now be crowded
down to a defile of just eight feet in width.

General Eblé spoke. "You have done more than enough,
Niellon. You shall command the demonstration at Borisow."

"No," said William. He, too, was of a sudden epic. Or
rather was it that, at the absolute limit of his strength, he was
ceasing to recognise himself? Or was he drunk on old
Armagnac?

William said: "I built a bridge over the Nile at Old Cairo.
Bérésina is but a trickle in comparison. My men shall build
the artillery-bridge."

Benthien, taciturn Saxon though he was, rose to the occasion. He said: "11th Company will build the foot-way. Nobody
else."

"When can you start, Captain Niellon?"

"Now." William gestured at the hamlet. "The gable posts will supply the uprights for the trestles and the wall-planks the deck. May I request that the buildings be strongly guarded while my men are at work?"

At 5 p.m., the pontonniers, assisted by a company of engineers, began taking down the houses.

The night was clear. Moon light flashed off the ice-blocks drifting down the stream. Straggle clouds, tinged red by the Russian camp fires, scudded over the firs on the far bank.

William thought: The engineering of timber bridges is not, in itself, or in times of security, a complex affair. Any trained engineer officer, sub-officer or veteran pontonnier can see, out of the half-dozen possibilities, which one has the best chance of success.

He will know that a fighting soldier, with his arms and equipment, weighs such and such, and six such men in marching order will weigh six times as much; a horse and rider such and such; a twenty-four-pound cannon such and such and a six-pound howitzer such; that a loaded wagon or caisson weighs such; and therefore the decking and trestles must be of such a bearing strength. He knows the co-efficient for the spacing of the uprights to give the greatest stability to the cross-beam, and also the breadth of the spans to permit the passage of trees uprooted by rains or, in the case here, blocks of ice broken in the thaw. The bridges must be close enough so that if one bridge-head is under enemy attack, the other will give means to reinforce it.

Into those elementary mathematics, war introduces a prodigious number of unknowns, like grit into a timepiece. Enemy action, the artillery rounds coming in every quarter-hour from the woods on the far bank, the great blocks of ice smashing into one another, the falling thermometer, the hunger of the men and the impatience of general officers combine to turn what should be simple into something of all but insuperable difficulty.

General Eblé was everywhere, murmuring orders, working with hammer and saw, a spray of nails in his teeth. Once he whispered: "Brave pontonniers! The eyes of the whole army are on us! Let us live up to the moment!" It seemed to William that, as at Smolensk, the men were glad to forget their misery in hard labour.

Sergeant Jeff, as always, had something to say.

"If we had brought just fifteen boats and their timber and teams, we would have had a bridge laid in an hour."

"We are where we are," said William.

XLIV

The next morning, Thursday, November 26th, 1812, at eight o'clock, they went into the water to erect the trestles, or, as we call them, *chevalets*. The shock of the water caused the men to curse, but the work was second nature. On land, during the night, they had nailed to each end of the transverse beam between the uprights a stringer. It was a matter of holding the uprights in place until the stringers could be attached to the completed section of the bridge and the unsquared logs, sixteen feet in length, laid for the deck. By good fortune, the frost had hardened the marsh on each bank. William divided what remained of the company into four, each division to work in the water for a half-hour.

As the day brightened, they came under fire from the far bank but the batteries on their side drove the Russian gunners back. A troop of cavalry went into the water, each horseman with an infantry skirmisher riding pillion. The fire coming in diminished and then stopped. William wondered if the feint at Borisow was succeeding. Jan, and then another man, slipped on the mud or simply gave in, and was swept downstream. The river-banks were strewn with corpses. Quite soon, William thought, I shall have no company left.

"Get out the fucking water, Willem."

As William stood by the fire, and his senses crept back, he felt a sensation akin to pleasure. If there was a single advantage to the cold of the Russian winter, it was that the lice that infested his clothes, underclothes, hair and beard ceased their activity at approximately the freezing point of water; but once their unwilling host came before a fire, they would wake from their brief hibernal slumber and return to their usual business of biting. William felt no discomfort. It was as if the Bérésina had washed the creatures away.

Scraps of conversation blew down at him.

"It is taking a very long time, General Eblé. A very long time."

"My people are up to their necks in water, Sire, with no food or brandy to warm them."

"Enough, sir!"

The Emperor stared at the ground and then looked up and round and fixed his glare on William.

"You, Mr Dutchman! Yes, you, sir! Complete the bridges this day and you shall be a baron of the Empire!"

William saluted, which caused the ice to fall from his cap.

The Emperor Napoleon wore a green velvet pelisse lined with sable, fur hat tied with black ribbons under the chin and sheep-skin boots. There was no good reason, after twenty-eight years, why he should recognise his class-mate. William was naked but for his drawers and undershirt, but the affront to military decency was more than concealed by a tight-fitting suit of black mud. William's right cheek and neck and his nose were black from frost-bite, his eyes blood-shot, and ice crusted on his moustaches and beard.

"It shall be done, Sire, the foot-bridge by noon, the artillery-way by dusk. I need no barony, Sire."

General Eblé had been humiliated, but he was not the

man to care. There was but one witness, and that was Niellon who cared even less.

Upstream, they could see the foot-way advancing in leaps. They had reached mid-stream, when a general officer shouted down at William.

"All men to work on the foot-way! Out of the water! Now!"

William put his head back and said: "If the men leave the water, they will not return. Also, this is my bridge until such moment as I hand it over to the army. You are trespassing, sir. Have the goodness to withdraw."

By good fortune, General Eblé appeared and took the enraged general officer back to the bank. (It was General Lauriston who, by a coincidence of no importance, was also Scottish by descent.)

"Every man to call out his name! In rotation."

With his passion for European uniformity, the Emperor had decreed that all of his Dutch subjects should have, like their French brothers and sisters, family names. The ordinance had yet to have its full effect.

"Gerrit, present!"

"Joris, present!"

"Jeff, less his bollocks!"

"Pieter, here!"

"Eblé, present!"

"Sir, for pity's sake, leave the water."

"Get the general out of the fucking river!"

General Eblé's face was white as paper. He shouted: "Pontonniers! I have never given an order that I would not carry out myself. In fifty years of service."

"Half up!"

"Every man out! And you, sir, also! Second detachment, make ready!"

Exact at noon, the upstream bridge was complete. To cries of joy and cheers, General Oudinot and the men of II Corps crossed over, the cavalrymen leading their horses, and took over the bridge-heads. At 4 p.m., as dusk was closing in, General Eblé handed over William's bridge. The II Corps artillery crossed first to support General Oudinot, then the guns of the Imperial Guard, and then the remainder of the park.

The great inconvenience of trestle bridges, and why bridges of boats and rafts are always to be preferred, is that, according to the condition of the river bed, the uprights respond in uneven fashion to the shock of the burden passing over them. The cross-beam moves out of the horizontal and the trestle loses its stability.

William shouted: "At the walk, gentlemen! At the walk!"

To no avail. At eight of the evening, three trestles collapsed. William and Eblé went to the bivouacs to lift the men. Money was of no more use than threats.

William said: "No bridge-builders have ever been faced

with such a task. Let us show the world and the ages to come what Dutchmen we were."

Sergeant Jeff shook the ice off his cape and stood up.

"Get up, you idle sods."

It snowed all night. Three hours were needed to repair the bridge but then, at 2 a.m, as the last of the guns were crossing, three trestles failed at the deepest part of the river. The men returned to the water, but they had become slow and heavy in their work, and nobody spoke. The feeling of progress, and the glimmer of survival, had left them. At 6 a.m on Friday, November 27th the bridge was open. The last of the guns crossed, and with them the heaviest shocks to the structure. At 10 a.m, the Guard crossed in good order, followed by the remains of Marshal Ney's troop, Davoust and Murat and Prince Eugène, and, shortly afterwards, the Emperor. The men swallowed some bouillon and slept standing, like cattle, by their fires.

William woke and did not recognise the world. In the falling snow, the riverbank was a mass of human beings, in thousands, vehicles of every description, and broken horses. They seemed to have come out of a dream.

Some were dressed in bear-skins, or peasants' caftanes, or pedlars' gabardines. William saw an immense grenadier in a lady's carriage-coat or *pelisse*, the pink satin trimmed with sable. Another man wore the cope of a priest of the Russian church, a third the quilted chapan of a Bokhara merchant. It was as if all the nations of Asia were in westward flight. On the heights above the mass of people, William could see men unlimbering cannon.

The mouths of the bridges were a mass of vehicles, stamping horses and shouting. Nobody would give way. Somebody hit a man across the face with his whip. The din was indescribable. Gendarmes, with the congenital pedantry of their profession, were letting only units intact and with their weapons onto the apron of the bridge. William understood that, in a beaten army, those without weapons are already casualties.

He met Captain Benthien half-way between the two bridges. That officer's problem was not the trestles, which were sound, but the constant shifting of the decking, so that those crossing were splashing through two feet of water. He feared that the weight of ice accumulating on the upstream face of the bridge must, in the end, break it.

Benthien told him that Marshal Victor, duc de Bellune, had established a weak rear-guard position on the slope. Exhausted, their clothes frozen stiff, and thinking themselves secure, the stragglers started fires and settled for the night in security. As far as William could judge, nobody crossed during the night.

He left the men by their fires, and himself repaired a broken section of deck in preparation for the crossing of the rear-guard guns.

*

The next morning, Saturday, November 28th, there was little movement. A sort of torpor had gripped the encampment. As the place stirred, and the fires were lit, William went round the bivouacs to encourage the people to cross.

Everywhere were helmets, shakos, cuirasses, smashed chests, shabraques, saddles. He saw silver ingots the size of house-bricks, icons, silver crucifixes, a jewel box with diamonds and spinels scattered in the snow. All about were the trophies that men had carried with them through their agony so that they could say to their grandchildren:

"*J'ai rapporté cela de Moscou.*"

I brought that back from Moscow.

Each treasure bore in itself the possibility of both life and posterity, and neither was now possible.

William saw things that no man should see nor describe for another to read. He saw men tumble down, blood oozing from their mouths. Another put a mitten to his nose, which came away in his hand. A third had crept for warmth into the belly of a slit horse and been garrotted as the flesh froze round his throat. He saw men hacking at the legs of a wounded comrade and throwing the dripping flesh into a cauldron. He saw a woman sprawled in the freezing mud, her skull split open by a gun-carriage wheel, and knew it was Mother Marietje.

This, thought William, is the hidden face of glory and is revealed only at rare moments. All of humanity's abstract values – glory, honour, chivalry, decency, piety – were devised to conceal the true circumstances of human existence. William smiled, which cracked the mud on his face, for he thought to have penetrated, in the last phase of his existence, the Inferno.

William had a thought, or rather an impression, that carried with it the ghost of a thought. None shall know of this shambles. History will say that the Emperor, in a position of peril that no commander had ever survived, beset to left and to right, and in the rear and ahead by Russian armies, yet had defeated them in detail and brought the effective part of the Grande Armée, his general officers, his Guard and his guns across the Bérésina river. His presence had inspired his army to prodigies of endurance while something in him not of this world, an aura of the uncanny, had stopped the Russians in their tracks or caused them to walk on tip-toe, like poachers in their own woods. None of the Russian commanders wished to be defeated by Napoleon Buonaparte. They would leave him to defeat himself and it would be his greatest victory.

Of the ineffective part of the Grande Armée, of the thousands of broken men without formation or weapons, and all the tailors, dancing-masters, pastry-cooks, masters-at-arms, opera dancers, hairdressers, grooms, lackeys – those apostles of French civilisation that Russia now had no more use for; all the mobs of *cantinières*, *vivandières* and camp-followers;

French, Germans, Portuguese, Croats, Romans, Neapolitans gathered up and dropped on this bloody marsh by the receding tide of M. Buonaparte's career; frozen in the snow, starved, burned in barns, gutted by mitraille or spitted by Cosaques; of them nothing shall be known for none shall live to tell the story. The Russians will say what they found on the banks of the Bérésina but none shall believe them.

This is the end, William thought. This empire, created like that of Alexander of Macedon in a fit of enchantment, like Alexander's without posterity or succession, will pass like Alexander's into myth.

A little after noon, from the heights behind Studianka, the Russian guns opened up. As the mortar shells burst across the encampment, there was a rush to the bridge-heads and, when those became clogged, men and women crowded the river's edge in a mass some six or seven hundred toises long and a hundred in depth. Whether by choice or because of the crush at their back, people were tumbling into the river, where they were carried by the stream or smashed senseless against the bridge-trestles. Below the bridges, the shores were a heap of dead bodies.

At the artillery-bridge, engineers were up-ending carriages and clearing the mob to make a sort of trench for the passage of Marshal Victor and his men. At each end of the bridges, the men had piled heaps of broken carts and timber, and set barrels of pitch, in preparation for their destruction once the rear-guard had passed. William sensed that Victor was under pressure, for round-shot and explosive were coming down amid the mob. Anyone falling was at once crushed under horses' feet.

At 9 p.m., what remained of Victor's force began to cross. William did not need to tell them to proceed at the walk. By 1 a.m. the last of the ambulant wounded had passed.

Marshal Victor said: "You may now fire the bridges, General Eblé."

"For pity's sake," said William, "give me two hours of daylight to get these people over."

"They will not cross. They must trust to the kindness of Russians."

"At 7.30 a.m.," General Eblé said, "the bridges will be fired at both ends."

"In one month, you shall be my guests at the Trois Frères," Marshal Victor said, and rode onto the bridge.

The survivors of William's company, twelve men, were gathered about a single fire.

"Men, you must cross now, or die here. The bridges will be burned at dawn."

Nobody answered.

Then Sergeant Jeff said: "We shall die like Dutchmen, smoking our pipes before a roaring fire."

There was a flicker of eye-lids for agreement.

Sergeant Jeff whispered: "Baron!"

William turned away.

XLV

Some time in the early morning of that Sunday, November 29th, small groups of Cosaques began to penetrate the crowd. Rather than approach the bridges, they seemed content to plunder the broken carriages and strewn corpses. The bombardment had ceased.

General Eblé said: "It is time, Niellon."

"I shall remain with my men."

"They are fallen, Captain Niellon."

"I must be sure of that."

A memory fluttered into his head and alighted. William said: "A partial success."

General Eblé turned and stepped on the bridge. His last words were: "Your name shall be known, Niellon, if I live, so help me."

William walked towards his men about the cold fire. His heart leaped when he saw them, huddled and upright, and the pipe-stub in Jeff's mouth. William shook his shoulder. It was hard as stone. The body fell away from him, like an antique statue rocked off its plinth. All were dead, petrified by the frost.

William went for the last time onto the bridge to signal to the men at the far end. Precisely, at mid-stream, he heard a feeble voice. Below him, a woman was clinging to the trestle upright. She had a baby slung across her breast.

"Take the child, sir! For God's sake, save the child!"

"The child will die without you. Hold on, if you are able, madame."

William dropped into the water. The woman was but skin and bone, and he was able to hoist her onto the decking. The child's lips were blue. Poor thing had but minutes of life left.

Looking back towards the east side, William saw the strangest of all the strange things he had seen. Waddling and shaking on the uneven roadway, a covered carriage was approaching at the walk. But for the mist of his breath, the coachman might have been a corpse. The reins were like sticks in his mittens.

William rapped on the *vasistas* or hatch behind the coachman. There was no answer. He pulled at the door. The inside was piled up with hay. In the space between the hay and the ceiling, William saw a bear-skin and three pairs of blood-shot eyes. Also, three pistols, pointed at his head.

William said: "If you shoot, you will be burned to cinders. Take the woman and child. They shall save you."

He bundled the new passengers into the hay, shut the carriage-door, stepped back and watched it sway and bump towards the land of France.

William had another thought, no more than a splinter. Could it be that everything in his life was preparation for this moment? Was it that only a man so far fallen in his estate, disappointed in love, nameless, friendless, past his youth, a non-entity, would carry out this trivial errand? To-night, the river will freeze and the Russian cavalry will cross at dawn and at ease. I have given the army but a half-dozen miles.

William took up a brand from the fire and dropped it into the barrel of pitch. The blast of heat on his face caused him to turn about. People were running at him. A great mass of human beings enveloped him. He fell. A body tumbled onto him, and then another and another, till there was but silence and darkness.

Captain Niellon's work was done.

"Will you show me that, father? I shall not take it from you."

The Cosaque showed the officer what was in his hand.

"Is the man alive?"

"He's on the short cut, Your Excellency."

The officer threw off his cape. "Place this over the man, Papa, and stay by him, and you shall have from me something of much more use to you than an old handkerchief. You shall have a great sum of money. And here is the instalment!"

The Cosaque caught the gold rouble in his cap.

The officer cantered, in his shirt, to the head of the head-quarters troop. The staff curvetted to block his passage, but our officer was by much the better horseman.

"Grace to speak, Sire!"

"You have earned it, Bielke."

"Grace to tend a wounded enemy officer, Sire!"

"Who is the officer, Count Bielke?"

"Neilson, Sire!"

"Canada Neilson's son?"

"General Neilson's grandson, Sire!"

"In victory, Count Bielke, there are no enemies. Only men. Granted."

PART 5

Deer's Glade

XLVI

William woke in a blast of light. Light was streaming through windows glazed with ice. But for his face, William was as warm as a new loaf of bread, muffled under something that felt like wool or fur. There was not a sound except, at a distance, the crash of an axe on wood and the clatter of horses' hooves. William did not know whether he was alive or dead but did not much care.

His head felt light and clean. He examined his right hand and saw it was wrapped in charpie and linen-bandage. With his left hand, he felt his hair had been cut to the scalp. His beard was shaved. His right cheek was smeared with some species of oil or fat.

He heard, speaking in Russian, a woman's voice that he seemed to have heard once before. Why was he in Russia? Is that the place of the dead? A lady put her head around the door. A little lower was a smaller head, and then two lower and smaller yet, and beneath the smallest that of a grey dog. William thought: Our notions of the after-life are crude, indeed.

"May we come in?"

"Of course," William said but made no sound. They came in, anyway.

William wondered whether it was modesty, or fear, that caused the lady to bring her children and dog with her. It did not occur to him, as it might to a father, that they were not entirely under their maman's orders.

The boy, who had on a miniature soldier's uniform, said: "Father said you saved the remnant of the Grande Armée."

"Did I?"

"You built the Berezin bridges and kept them open. You and your brave pontonniers."

William began to weep. It was as if, having shed the burden of his life, he must now take it up and crawl on.

Yet this life was not so very bad, to have survived and be in the same room as the woman he loved. William said to himself: Is this my portion of happiness? I would have settled for less.

"What is this place?"

"Olenskaïa Polana. Deer's Glade."

Deer's Glade! William had come into a world of light and fur, children and hounds. Winter sunlight blazed through the glass-doors, and passing through it in gusts of light, happy, rich, beloved of her children, was Isabelle. (Even William could hear that her Russian was as bad as her German.) If Isabelle had been sad, or dull, or sick for France, or shunned by her neighbours, or robbed by her intendant, William might have borne it, but more probably not. He did not believe that in a thousand years he might make any woman happy.

The house was packed to the rafters with unlucky relations and superannuated servants. Sometimes they came to his room to peer at him. Once, William woke to see at the end of his bed an old soldier with his moustaches in a net. William greeted him. The gentlemen pointed to the net and then to his mouth, which stayed closed. The girls, who were called Anna and Sonya, erected their doll's houses in diagonal corners. William could hear them soothing, scolding and bandaging their waxen patients. At evening, when Isabelle read prayers in the room to the whole house, William was all but suffocated by the smells of farm, lower-court and kitchen.

Young Kolia had followed every stage and action of the campaign, and was eager to inform William.

"Then the Emperor, the Guard, the head-quarters staff with Mme Fusil of the Moscow Opéra, Marshal Ney, Davoust, Prince Eugène and finally the duc de Bellune, General Victor. Once the rear-guard was over, those without arms or formation were called up but few chose to cross.

The bridges on the left bank were burned under heavy fire by Captain Niellon. I mean, by you, sir, at seven o'clock . . .

"Nine o'clock. How many, dear Kolia?"

"At Wilna, General Eblé and thirty Dutch and Poles. General Eblé succumbed to typhus at Königsberg."

"I killed my men."

"Father says the Emperor killed your men, Captain. What made His Imperial Majesty think that he could conquer Russia!"

XLVII

Back at midsummer, when Count Bielke sent word that the French had crossed the Niemen, Isabelle went out at midnight and threw the standard from Austerlitz into the back-courtyard well. The cattle, sheep, horses and young girls she hid in a wooded ravine, just as when Charles of Sweden had marched into the district a hundred years before. She kept only the worn-out dairy cows, the jaded horses and the scrapie sheep.

When the French foraging party arrived, looking evil, she greeted the officer in command from the terrace. She said she was a Frenchwoman from Orléans who would be delighted with the company of her countrymen at dinner. The other ranks would be entertained in the dairy. She asked only that,

in the house, as the floors were rotten, the gentlemen take off
their boots.

"Why their boots?"

"Men cannot do much harm in their stockinged feet."

William laughed.

"You are laughing?"

"Am I?"

Once the feast was done, the French took six dry cows,
five dozen sheep, eight bullocks and four carts of hay. They
promised to return the wagons and horses, but did not.

At Christmas, the children staged tableaux of biblical
scenes. William was a triumph as the Risen Lazarus, ascending to Kolia's outstretched palm like iron to a magnet, the
tapes unravelling and falling from his face and hands, caus-
ing one of the kitchen-girls to scream. Sometimes the room
was so warm that William saw through his heavy eyes
mother, gouvernante, house-tutor, children and dog all
asleep. The sound of their snores, each at a different pitch,
had the character of a symphony.

Anna, the youngest child, who knew no German, had a
mind to teach William Russian, while Isabelle sat in the
corner, sewing or writing her letters or balancing accounts.

"How many fingers have I?"

"Seven?"

"Wrong."

"Seven and one half?"

"Correct. How many toes?"

"Anna!"

"Please, madame. Let us proceed with the lesson. How many toes have I?"

Anna looked away.

"Ten?"

"Nine?"

"Eight?"

Isabelle cried out: "William, Count Bielke saved your legs. Is not that something? Petia! You wicked hound, get off Captain Neilson's bed!"

The dog raised a heavy head. He looked at the countess as if to say: "With the greatest respect, my lady, is that not for the Captain to determine?"

"Oh, for the love of God, I have no authority in this house."

The dog went back to sleep.

After they had gone, William rose and taught himself to walk on five toes, three and two.

XLVIII

In the new year of 1813, William stepped down from his bed. The family's general quarter transferred to the winter garden. Outside, beneath the snow imprinted by birds' feet, William could make out the lines of parterres and walks. To make himself useful, William sat in the stove-light and cut from elm-wood playthings and saints for the children, while Petia dozed at his feet. They played Cat and Mouse, William always the cat, but the children on their sylphid feet eluded him. By reason of his injuries, the children had no fear of him.

At night, William slept little. He wrote from his empty head his report of the march from Moscow to the river. At the first sound of feet from below, he rose and put on his robe and cap. In the dark enfilade of rooms, a house-maid padded away with a candle-stub that caused shadows to prance on wall and ceiling. Before giant tiled stoves men crouched like demons, feeding the flame with billets of pine which spat and bubbled. The morning-room was red with stove-light. Exhausted by his journey, William sat down and stared into the flames. Here, thought William, I could pass my life, looking into fire.

In reality, the patient was waiting for a sound; and it was coming, a commotion in the back court, shouts, curses, bumps, stumbles, scratches on wood and claws skidding on board, and Petia's front paws on his knees and tongue on his chin. After so great a commotion, once sure that his friend had survived their separation, the animal lay down to sleep across William's feet.

In the evenings, Isabelle and William sat beside the lamp and tea-machine or *samovar*. She inhabited the room as if it were her clothing. Tables, chairs, pictures, busts, glass doors: all had something of her nature or were that nature itself. Even the Gardner tea-cups were there to console. Each object seemed to say to William: You have read your Plato. We are not what you want but we are not nothing.

Isabelle spun, a pile of fleeces by her chair. (For reasons none could remember, Count Bielke's grandmother, Countess Lidia, had settled several families of Persians on a corner of her lands and built them a shrine for their worship. Expert in weaving floor-rugs, horse-trappings, cushions, bolsters, saddle-bags and purses, the immigrants had a great need of wool yarn. The winter months were thus given over to spinning, with Isabelle leading by example.)

William marvelled at the gift of women in general, and Isabelle in particular, to make so commonplace an occupation graceful. When the aunts and cousins crept in, lured by the tea-steam like the Olympian gods to sacrifice, Isabelle banished them with a softness that was, none the less, implacable. William understood that Isabelle no longer feared that he might break the truce. They spoke very little, but every now and then, Isabelle might say:

"Do you remember the ascent in the aerostat?"

"How could I forget it, Isabelle?"

"And M. Fleurant?"

"I am afraid he is no longer living."

"Poor man. Did he fall to earth?"

"Yes. One morning, in 1808 or 9, coming out of his house in the rue des Petits Champs, he slipped on his top step, fell and broke his head."

"Oh, William, it's caught again!"

"Don't move. I'll set the wheel."

Isabelle said: "Poor M. Fleurant. He never made his peace with gravity."

William laughed.

XLIX

On the next post-day, Isabelle burst in with a letter. She was in floods of tears.

"I know it is from maman but it is in cipher!"

"May I see it, countess?"

Isabelle showed the cover, but kept good hold of it. The surface was scrawled with every sort of mark and stamp, including that of the Imperial Post at Odessa.

"It is not in cipher, countess. It is in Arabic. I was some time in Egypt and the Holy Land. May I try to read it to you?"

Isabelle looked doubtful, even envious, but broke the seal and relinquished the paper.

The Arabic script is so beautiful that some writers forget their intention to inform, and sacrifice legibility to elegance. William had often found that unless he already knew what was being written, such as a verse of the Alcoran, he could only admire.

That was not the case here. The script was as clear as water.

William began. "In the name of God, the merciful, the compassionate, from the meanest of His servants to her beloved daughter Ezabel, pride of womanhood and morning-star of virtue, peace!

"By the grace of God the Almighty, and the beneficence of Abou Mohammed Hammouda bin Ali Pacha, viceroy of Tunis, Lord of Carthage and Commander of the Faithful, this servant lives in retirement in the city of Tunis, engaged in the perfection of the Arabian tongue and the study of the religious sciences."

"My maman is a Turk!" Isabelle was both laughing and crying.

"It may be prudent dissimulation on the lady's part, the which, in at least one of their schools of law, may, on occasion, be meritorious."

"Nonsense. Maman never does anything by half."

Isabelle looked a moment downcast. "Will Maman be permitted to travel?"

"She shall, madame, by the leave of her guardians, who are my father and Count Bielke. I believe my father shall accord his sister every latitude . . ."

". . . and Count Bielke is afeared of her."

Isabelle sprang up and cried:

"We have come through!"

"Isabelle! Do not say such things!"

Isabelle was dancing. "Hourra! Hourra! We have come through."

Countess Bielke was gliding over the floor. Then, seeing that only Petia the dog was matching her steps, Isabelle paused and caught her breath.

"And so many as good or better have fallen down. Why have we, not they, survived?"

"I do not know, countess."

They were falling back into their old closeness. Grief is a royal road, thought William. Time to gather up the bits and pieces of the soul and set off into futurity.

William read on:

"There is word in the city that the Emperor of the French – May God hasten his demise! – has taken a great army into the Kingdom of Rus. All day and night, I pray that your cousin William shall not come to harm. Write if you can to your loving mother in the charge of the custodian of the Hammouda Pacha mosque at Tunis and you will staunch a bleeding heart."

William returned the letter.

"What will happen, William?"

"The Emperor will abdicate. The Tsar, who has a kindness for him, will give him Corsica to rule. He shall have a Life

Guard and an artillery park and fortifications and good laws and sound money. Perhaps it had been better for all if he had never left that island."

Isabelle may have remarked the politics in those sentences, as also the Mohammedan jurisprudence earlier, and thought to see a widening in her patient's mental horizon. She said: "May I write to my maman to say that you are recovered from your wounds?"

"Of course, madame."

"And that you shall return to France as soon as you are fully restored?"

"I would prefer if you did not."

Isabelle's eyes swam with tears.

"That is desertion, William."

"Yes."

There was nothing to say. What could William say? That, in saving his life, Pavel Sergueïevitch had done him no kind of service. What could Isabelle say? That they were where they were and that was that.

He said: "I have written a letter to Pavel Sergueïevitch. You would oblige me, countess, if you would give it to him at his furlough."

"You shall not wait to thank him."

"No."

Isabelle looked away. She said to air: "What will you do with the life he gave you?"

"Live it."

What could William say? That in finding Isabelle here, in her nimbus of happiness and honour, he would have her descend to share his misery? All day and night, he listened to the bumping of blocks of ice as they came down the Dnieper. He could feel the house withdrawing as on tip-toe from the winter guest.

Except little Anna.

They spoke in Russian sentences from the primer.

"Shall His Excellency travel far?"

"He shall go whither the road shall have taken him."

"Shall His Excellency travel alone or with a companion?"

"He shall take the road sole and alone. Good children care for their parents."

The house filled with hyacinths forced in the hot-house. The scent of artificial spring blowing at him from every table made William restless. He was impatient to be on his way. He had gained a taste for suffering.

William cleaned the rust from his sabre and, with his own hand in the smithy, put an edge on the blade, while the horse-troughs overflowed in the endless rain. One night, on his bed-side table, William saw the blazoned handkerchief, washed, darned, hemmed and pressed.

L

The children stood in spring sunshine at the foot of the steps, like dabs of light. Before them, Petia the dog was seated on his haunches, turning his head to the house and then to William, back and forth. William bent to shoulder his pack and take up his stick. Isabelle spoke in Russian. The dog rose in a spiral, again and again and again; and then sprang towards William and took station at his left heel. William turned and raised his arm in farewell.

William Neilson felt ground beneath his feet.

He said: "Now, good Petia, you shall mend your pace to mine. Say farewell, for neither dogs nor men live long."

To be continued.

RAISING READERS

Books Build Bright Futures

Dear Reader,

We'd love your attention for one more page to tell you about the crisis in children's reading, and what we can all do.

Studies have shown that reading for fun is the **single biggest predictor of a child's future success** – more than family circumstance, parents' educational background or income. It improves academic results, mental health, wealth, communication skills and ambition.

The number of children reading for fun is in rapid decline. Young people have a lot of competition for their time, and a worryingly high number do not have a single book at home.

Our business works extensively with schools, libraries and literacy charities, but here are some ways we can all raise more readers:

- Reading to children for just 10 minutes a day makes a difference
- Don't give up if your children aren't regular readers – there will be books for them!
- Visit bookshops and libraries to get recommendations
- Encourage them to listen to audiobooks
- Support school libraries
- Give books as gifts

Thank you for reading.
www.JoinRaisingReaders.com